T·H·E
WOODEN
HEART

The Wooden Heart

by LaJoyce Martin

©1991 Word Aflame Press
Hazelwood, MO 63042-2299
Reprint History: 1996

Cover Design by Tim Agnew
Cover Art by Art Kirchhoff

All Scripture quotations in this book are from the King James Version of the Bible unless otherwise identified.

All rights reserved. No portion of this publication may be reproduced, stored in an electronic system, or transmitted in any form or by any means, electronic, mechanical, photocopy, recording, or otherwise, without the prior permission of Word Aflame Press. Brief quotations may be used in literary reviews.

Printed in United States of America

Printed by

Library of Congress Cataloging-in-Publication Data

Martin, LaJoyce, 1937–
    The wooden heart / LaJoyce Martin.
      p.   cm.
    ISBN 0-932581-85-4 :
    I. Title.
PS3563.A72486W6   1991
813'.54--dc20   91-11965
                                                                CIP

Other Books by LaJoyce Martin:

The Harris Family Saga:
To Love a Bent-Winged Angel
Love's Mended Wings
Love's Golden Wings
When Love Filled the Gap
To Love a Runaway
A Single Worry
Two Scars Against One
The Fiddler's Song

Pioneer Romance Series:
So Swift the Storm
So Long the Night

Pioneer Romance:
The Wooden Heart
Heart-Shaped Pieces
Light in the Evening Time

Western:
The Other Side of Jordan
To Even the Score

Path of Promise:
The Broken Bow
Ordered Steps

Children's Short Stories:
Batteries for My Flashlight

Nonfiction:
Mother Eve's Garden Club
Heroes, Sheroes, and a Few Zeroes

Order from:
Pentecostal Publishing House
8855 Dunn Road
Hazelwood, MO 63042-2299

Dedicated to:
Barbara Murphy
A lady with a true pioneer spirit.

Contents

Chapter 1	The Heart on the Tree	9
Chapter 2	The Storm	15
Chapter 3	The Letter	23
Chapter 4	New Neighbors	31
Chapter 5	The Drifter	39
Chapter 6	Trouble at the Well	47
Chapter 7	Mr. Webster's Surprise	55
Chapter 8	The Death of a Dream	65
Chapter 9	The Journal	73
Chapter 10	The Listener	79
Chapter 11	Mrs. Trouble	87
Chapter 12	A New Worry	97
Chapter 13	The Wings	105
Chapter 14	Julius	113
Chapter 15	The Revelation	121
Chapter 16	Teacher Conference	127
Chapter 17	The Ultimatum	135
Chapter 18	The Rosebud	141
Chapter 19	A Way Out	149
Chapter 20	The Teacher's Call	157
Chapter 21	A Trip to Town	163
Chapter 22	Framed!	171
Chapter 23	The Two-Timer	177
Chapter 24	The Accident	183
Chapter 25	Back to the Well	189
Chapter 26	The Anniversary	195
Chapter 27	A Changed Boy	201
Chapter 28	The Third Event	207
Chapter 29	Laying down the Law	215
Chapter 30	Fevered Confession	223
Chapter 31	Keeping a Promise	229

CHAPTER ONE

The Heart on the Tree

I can't give you up, Daniel!

Ellie Webster's wet cheek lay hard against the heart-shaped scar whittled deep in the bark of the tree that arched over the trail. With that pitiful sob, her arms tightened around the oak's insensitive trunk as if by clinging to it she could hold her lost love.

After half a decade, the carved heart that fenced his initials and hers still gave testimony to their young romance. Neither time nor weather had erased it.

She had been sixteen then. Sixteen, and too caught up in the moment to take a thought of the future, blind to the winds of fate that banked black clouds for tomorrow's storm.

"What a fool I am!" she cried, raining more tears upon the tree. "I have not heard a word from him in five years. I should give up! But giving up one's dream isn't easy...."

A leaf fluttered down and lodged in her hair as if to offer solace. A squirrel, pirouetting from limb to limb,

stopped statue still to study this picture of dejection.
It was a quiet morning; the whole atmosphere awaited summer's dying breath. Even the birds sang pianissimo. Once Ellie's heart had sung along with the field thrushes. Was that five summers—or an eternity—ago? The walk to the limestone well for water brought a thrill then. Now the journey never failed to remind her of that last look into Daniel Brock's clear brown eyes.

Here in memory's wake, Ellie's mind could find no defined birth of the courtship. Was her affection for him born the day he opened his syrup bucket and shared his lunch with her when her own lunch sack was stolen? He was in the third grade, she in the first. She could almost taste the stringy ham between the top and bottom of the flat biscuit. Or was it boyish concern she tasted?

Or did the first flame of romance start on the creek bank as he baited her hook during those adolescent years when time suspended a body between childhood and adulthood? Or when he picked cockleburs from her mittens to save her own hands the pain? Or when he talked to her about God . . . and what was good and right and honest?

As she reflected upon it now, it seemed that Daniel diffused into her life like a slow summer sunset. And as beautifully. She never questioned her love for him. It was just—there.

Sometimes it seemed but yesterday that they stood by their tree looking into each other's eyes. Then, at other times, it seemed a thousand milleniums in the past.

"Ellie," Daniel had said that day, "next to God, I love you more than anyone. Someday I will marry you, and we will be together forever." While he talked, he formed the heart on the tree with his pocketknife and linked the

letters together inside its perimeter as a sort of unspoken proposal. Ellie's wide violet eyes, framed with their smoky lashes, spoke more than her mouth ever could have said.
Oh, Daniel! There'll never be anyone else. . . .
Why hadn't he told her that this etched heart was his farewell gesture? That his family planned to join the wagon train to go west the very next day? Surely he had known!

Ellie pressed her face harder against the tree in a futile effort to block out the mental picture and lock it away from memory's prowling fingers. But her stubborn heart would drag it out again: Daniel's guileless smile, Daniel's bronzed face, Daniel's laughing eyes, Daniel's broad shoulders.

Had he really cared, he would have come to me before he left or at least left a message. He would have returned for me by now, her mind niggled, but her heart flew to his defense. He *did* mean it when he said he loved me! Oh, I know he meant it then! His eyes were true. But he has . . . forgotten.

Can love forget? mocked a demon of logic.

Life had hosted many changes since Daniel's going, changes that cost Ellie bitter heartaches. When she was eighteen, her mother died, leaving her to manage the household for her father and four younger (and thoughtless) brothers. One by one, life's anchors snapped without warning. All the scabbed-over wounds broke open and bled. She was sore hearted, numb, frightened. The keel of her ship lay splintered and strewn.

Now she felt like an old woman rolling a great stone endlessly uphill. Days and nights meshed into a whirlpool of thankless work and less affection. Her father was a hard man, her brothers careless. Aside from her mother's Bible and her dream of Daniel, she had but broken fragments to cling to.

A cow bawled in the distance, bringing an answer from another, a reminder that it would soon be milking time. Recalled to present duties, Ellie unwound herself from the tree and picked up the empty wire-handled bucket. Grim determination set her jaw; she hurried on to the well, filled the container with water, and started for home.

When still a small silhouette with her burden bumping along beside her, splashing onto her petticoats, Ellie became the subject of her brothers' prattle.

"Why do you s'pose Ellie hates goin' to the well so?" The two boys pushed and pulled the gap-toothed saw, tormenting the wood they worked on.

"I never paid no mind, really."

"Well, mind next time she starts that direction. She'll use any excuse she's got or make up a new one to get outta goin' for water."

"Mayhap it sads her to think on leavin' the house and goin' back without Maw there. Maw's apoplexy was so suddenlike and unexpected, it made her more mawkish than she a'ready was. She ain't never quit grieving over Maw, I think. I guess girls is just different than boys."

"My remembering goes back afore Maw died. Ellie hated worser than thunder goin' for water even when Maw was still livin'. Fer a fact, most time Maw went to the well herself 'cause she knew Ellie hated the chore so bad."

"Mayhap she's afretted of poison ivy. Poison ivy vines grows all down by the well and on both sides of the trail. She had it once afore. And it sure ain't no fun gettin' the itch and blisters."

"She wouldn't have no worries of the vines except in spring and summer, would she?"

"Mayhap she's scared of snakes. Most girls is."

"You sure ain't been mindin'. She goes to the crick without a blink of the eye. And to the woodpile. And to the henhouse to gather eggs. There'd be no less snakes one direction than t'other. Snakes don't all congregate at a well. They'd as lief haunt the henhouse. Besides, snakes put theirselves up for the winter, and she hates the well just as bad in the winter as she does in the summer. Mayhap even a little worser."

"Mayhap the wire handles hurts her hands."

"Jimmy Webster! She brings up the buckets filled with milk from the cow milkin' every mornin' and every evenin'. If it was a matter of heavy buckets, it would show up somewhere else in bucket liftin'. Is water weightier than milk? Now answer me that if you're so smart."

Travis gave the saw a wicked yank, almost throwing Jimmy off balance. Jimmy spat an oath he had heard at school.

"Well then, mayhap she's just lazy. And if you think *I'm* goin' to offer to bring up the water in her place . . ."

"Peculiar she is, but I'd never lay a lazy blame to Ellie. Who is it that does all our cookin' and warshin' and ironin' but Ellie herself? Besides the milkin' and churnin' and egg gatherin'?"

"Mayhap . . ."

"Hush! You're just mayhapin' for the sake of mayhapin'. And your mayhaps don't even make horse sense. If you can't give better reasonin' than you've been givin', quit botherin'."

"If you didn't want my mayhapin', why did you lift the subject and ask me for, then? Huh? I ain't never been keen on what goes on inside the heads of women. They have scrambled-up notions. They're all strange if'n you ask me. I ain't never goin' to take one to wife!"

"Hoity-toity! That's what they all say! Some little button-nose sweetie will come along some day and . . . "

"Shut up!"

Travis coughed to warn Jimmy of Ellie's approach, and the subject dropped.

Ellie hurried, almost tripping over the same snag of root that caught her foot only yesterday. Some of the water in the bucket splashed out, a greater anguish to her than her stubbed toe. Water lost meant trips to the well more often. And a trip to the well meant going by the tree with its heart-shaped memorial. The cut that bore her initials. And his. Must hurts hurt forever?

I'll live and die with my dream, and nobody but God will ever know why I loathe going to the well for water. Every trip brings back the raw pain. . . .

Travis watched her through narrowed eyes. But the mystery of his sister's frown was sealed—and might forever be sealed—within her own soul.

CHAPTER TWO

The Storm

"*P*ack me a lunch, too, Ellie." Mr. Webster took one last gulp from the granite dipper and then gave it a rude toss back into the bucket. Ellie heard it splash and settle to the bottom. "I'm going to Springdale on business. I'll be gone the day."

Whether it was the smell of mothballs that made Ellie turn around to look at her father or the strained casualness of his voice, she could not have told. But what she saw gave her a start.

Her father carried a strange look in his steel gray eyes. He wore his black serge suit, its frock coat buttoned tightly across a thickening waistline. It had been his wedding suit, expanded after a few years by a V-shaped inset in the back to compensate for the many helpings of biscuits and gravy.

Crease lines from the wooden hanger announced that the suit had not been worn since his wife's funeral three years before. His black felt hat was as outdated as his high double collar. Ellie noticed that he had even waxed his moustache for the trip.

What sort of business would warrant such attire? She almost asked the question, but bit her tongue just in time. Silently she cut the meat thinner to accommodate five lunches instead of the usual four, skimping on young Walter's sandwich. She added an extra sugar cookie to his flour sack as compensation.

It was the first day of school, a day she had anticipated since the dismissal of classes three months earlier. And now with her father fettered in some unknown business, she would have the whole of the day to herself. She could follow her heart.

Scarcely were Mr. Webster and her brothers out of sight when she snatched off her faded apron and reached for her bonnet. Then, in a near run, she headed for the Brock place, picking her way through the brush and paying little heed to the briars that grabbed at her stockings. Better the snags than taking a chance of being seen.

She heaved a sigh, the sound a mixture of dread and pleasure. Each summer stretched longer than the one before; her days filled with hungry boys to feed, boys who would question her absence for a single hour. She had not made the trip to the Brock farm since May when the roses were in bloom. Time stalled throughout the summer days. Now the clock ticked again; she was on her way to Daniel's home place.

These secret pilgrimages began the spring after Daniel left. Ellie slipped away now and then to weed Mrs. Brock's flowers. As she patted fresh dirt around them, quenching their thirst from the hand pump, she reasoned that a well-kept yard would be a welcome blessing to come home to. A strange analogy existed between the survival of the flowers and her own dreams.

The second year, she grew brave enough to pull the mask off her motives, bringing them to task. *This is how a moth must feel,* she thought, *torn from his cocoon, his cast disclosed, facing the glare of reality.*

"I'm on no good Samaritan mission for Daniel's mother." She said it aloud so that there was no escaping her own rebuke. "Daniel loved bringing me clippings from his mother's plants. I want to keep the flowers alive for him . . . and for me. So that someday he will bring me another bouquet."

The next April—the year her mother died—the yard work provided a therapy. The forsaken property became her citadel, a place to think and pray, away from her own mother-abandoned home.

And now, nurturing the plants was a part of her existence, like tending the grave of a loved one. There was no good reason, but she supposed she would be fighting away the choking weeds barehanded until the earth claimed her body and God claimed her soul. And each year she picked a single rose as a tribute to her lost love.

It had been an especially dry year; the spring showers were stingy. In sight of the cottage, Ellie caught her breath at the graybeards that hung like dried straw. The larkspur was a mass of shriveled pods. The weeds, though, thrived and dominated. She saw that she had much work to do and at the yard's edge fell to her knees with a cry of distress. *It will be a full day's job. I should have brought along a lunch for myself,* she thought.

A line of flat stones made a path to the front entrance. Beside the walkway, brittle stems clung to the roots beneath them for life. Working her way toward the house,

Ellie stopped, pursing her lips. Several of the plants were hopelessly crushed, as if something heavy had been dropped on them. Shoots and stalks were broken, forever robbed of blooms. What could have happened?

She clawed and yanked at the weeds until her hands burned, red and raw. Something of the contest against the enemy of the sweet blossoms gave her a determination as unrelenting as the weeds themselves. They would not take the roses . . . the jonquils . . . the morning glories! Time could not take her memories . . . her fleeting happiness . . . her dreams!

An hour passed. Then another. Had Ellie looked up, she would have seen the greenish-black formations that swallowed more and more of the sky. But she sensed nothing until the first roll of thunder banged from cloud to cloud. A twisted thread of lightning burned through the heavens. She raised her head in time to see a wall of solid water moving toward her. What should she do?

Before they went away, the Brocks had boarded up their house. A glance toward the front door told Ellie that the guardian boards had not miraculously rotted away; they were still there. She could not hope to gain entrance to the building.

The rush of rain and the roar of wind pounded her ears. From the direction it traveled, she would need to seek protection behind the house—if she could find protection at all. The back stoop lay beneath a short overhang. It wouldn't help much, but any haven was better than none.

With her skirts gathered about her legs, Ellie made a dash around the building, falling onto the small back porch. A droplet of rain kicked up the dust at her feet, followed by a mad race of other anxious divers. She decided she was in the best place possible.

All at once, the rain slacked to a sinister lull. A gust of wind whipped around the eaves, its chilliness a surprise. Hail! Panic tore at Ellie's throat. Rain was one thing, but anywhere outside was not shelter enough from flying hail.

The outhouse! If she could make it to the outhouse! But there was no time. And worse yet, if she did reach the privy, it might topple in the wind, claiming her as its prisoner. She shook her head to clear her thoughts of such a horror.

In her confusion, she threw an imploring look toward the back door. If she could get inside . . . Why—why—! She looked again, afraid that she might be hallucinating. The restraining boards were *gone*. They had been removed, and the door stood open a full inch or more.

With a prayer of thanks, she scrambled inside as the first ball of hail crashed against the roof. Safe! She was safe! She fell against the wall with a half laugh, half cry. For a few moments, she heard nothing, felt nothing but relief. Then she looked around. A thin shaft of light fell across the worn linoleum, revealing the arch-shaped pattern in the dust where the door had been opened. Someone had been here! Someone had *pushed* the door open! And recently. Ellie's heart leaped. *Could it . . . might it have been a member of Daniel's family?* She followed the light to its source and saw that the pull-down shade that once covered the south window was raised.

She almost felt that someone was in the house now. Further examination showed footprints that crossed and crisscrossed the floor in the dust. She peered into each dusky room but found no one there.

Except for the missing items of furniture that the Brocks must have taken west with them, nothing was changed from the way she remembered the interior of the house. She would indulge herself this once . . . and pretend she was sixteen again. . . . Her mind reached back beyond her bleached-out dreams, back to the tree. She squeezed her eyelids together to choke off unwanted tears and to envision Daniel's hand as it carved:

D.B.
+
E.W.

The howling of the storm grew wilder as Ellie sat in the chair to wait out the storm. Bold hopes dared to crowd into the familiar room with her. Hopes that she had tethered many times only to have them jerk loose and gallop about her causing her heart to race faster and faster. *Someone has been here. Could it be that he will return!*

But surely if Daniel still held plans for me, he would have made some effort to contact me long before now, she argued with herself, hating the reality that disturbed her fantasy. She lived with the bald truth all year long. Why could not this one day be hers to daydream?

Thoughts of the young romance pushed warm blood to her neck and ears. *Oh, Daniel! I loved you so!*

Her mind backed up and went forward, started and stopped until there was no pattern at all to the maze of deliberation that came and went. She tried to herd her scattered thoughts into one pen and keep them there, but like slippery pigs breaking through the pigsty, they darted away just when she had them corralled. With the heel of her blistered hand, she pounded her forehead to clear her thinking.

It had been such a strange day. Why had her father put on the funeral suit to go into town? The way he held his head and his voice all framed a complex mystery. Had it any connection with the open door, the raised shade, the footprints? What did it all mean?

A thrashing black spider swung from its single strand of web, twirling in the air and displaying the telltale orange spot on its belly. A black widow! It fell to the floor, and Ellie jumped up, intent on killing the poisonous arachnid. But the spider slid under the edge of the tattered, braided rug that banked against the front threshold.

Ellie jerked the rug back with one quick motion and stamped on the spider with her foot. As she pulled the mat from the door, a dust-covered envelope that had been imprisoned by the rug fell at her feet. It had to be a letter the Brocks dropped on their way out.

She picked it up to place it on the table for them in the event they should return. Suddenly the room swam out of focus and back again. *Her own name was on the letter!* And in the upper left-hand corner was Daniel Brock's name in his own handwriting.

CHAPTER THREE

The Letter

A chair caught Ellie's falling body. Her knees buckled, too weak to hold her weight. She still clung to the envelope, her hands trembling.

"Daniel!" she whispered, a film of tears making his handwriting blur and dim. "Oh, Daniel, you *did*—"

The pounding of heavy boots at the back door made her fold her sentiment in half. Someone was coming! She stuffed the precious letter into the bodice of her dress and sucked in her breath. Who knew that she was here? Had one of her brothers or her father followed her? And if so, for what reason?

The boots stamped in mud-ridding, water-shaking thuds that vibrated the whole house. Ellie looked about wildly. How could she escape without being seen? The front door was boarded up and the window nailed shut. She felt like a trapped animal, cowering and caught.

When the square-jawed hulk of a man appeared, he froze in his tracks. His puzzled look suggested that he couldn't decide whether the girl sitting in this deserted house was an apparition, a stone statue, or a mortal. He stepped back quickly, begging her pardon for the intrusion. "P-pardon me. I-I thought this house was . . . e-empty," he stammered.

Ellie found her voice coming from a tight, dry throat. "Usually it is, sir. I was just in the yard . . . on the back stoop, that is, and . . . and. . . ." She didn't know how much to say and how much to leave unsaid. She reasoned that she was at the mercies of this stranger, so she would be as tractable as possible and hope that he would not harm her. And yet, her reasons for being here were none of his business.

"Then you don't live here, miss?" The thick man, Ellie noted, had a dome of rust-colored hair that receded from his forehead, giving the illusion that the whole of it had slid backward a few inches. His unkempt beard and brushy eyebrows seemed to be tie-dyed to match his hair.

"No, sir."

"I guess you got caught in the wretched storm like I did. I holed up in a lean-to out there, but got mighty fearful the thing would cave in on me when the wind kicked up a fuss. Whew! But I'm glad it's over. Do you have these hail-splitting fits of weather in this part of the country often?"

Ellie's thoughts had been so blotted up with Daniel's letter that she never knew when the sky cast off its flannel-gray cloak and the sun crept out again. She looked toward the window in surprise. "It has been a rather extraordinary summer. All spring it was dry. This storm was—suddenlike. Normally the weather isn't so violent."

"I wouldn't have barged in if I had known anyone was here," the man apologized again. "My name is Greaves.

Old man Greaves. I had been in the house looking around earlier and found it empty, swept, and garnished. I was about to decide to bring in seven more worse than myself," he chuckled at his own distorted humor. "And we'd all move in."

"Oh, you couldn't do that, sir."

"I was just looking this neck of the woods over, thinking on locating down here. I hail from about two hundred mile upcountry. I was taking a look around this vacant house when the cloudburst came up. Would you by chance, know the people who own this piece of property?"

"Yes, sir. Their name is Brock. They went out west some time ago."

"Do you know if they would be interested in selling the property?"

"Oh, I'm sure they wouldn't!"

"Do they return to check on their property now and then?"

Ellie felt uncomfortable with the questions Mr. Greaves asked. "I—don't really know, sir."

"But as far as you know, they ain't never returned?" His piercing eyes made her squirm.

"I expect they'll be back any day now."

"Isn't there some law in this state that says if property owners don't pay their taxes for a certain number of years, the land can be turned over to others who will pay up the back taxes?"

"I've not studied up on the laws, sir. But I'm sure the Brocks have kept their taxes paid."

"The place looks a bit run down and neglected."

"I take care of the flower beds."

"Well, I sure like this place, and I'd like to get my

hands on it. I think Mazie would like it, too. Mazie's my *now* wife. I used to be married to Bonny Jean, but she skipped out with our hired man. That gave me excuse enough to divorce her. Mazie's younger and more my type, anyhow.

"We had six youngsters, me and Bonny. All of them boys. Jed was the oldest; then there was Alvin and Hershel and Cory and Otis and Eddy. Mazie's first man—she wasn't married very long to him—had a grown-up son. He laid out all night and nooned in for grub and wanted to eat at mine and Mazie's table. I put a stop to that right quick.

"Now me and Mazie have a baby girl of our own. It's a mine-and-ours mixup. You see, Bonny won't leave us alone to our own lives where we live now, even though she and her new man have two kids now. So I thought it would be best for me and Mazie to hightail it as far away as we could get." He paused to study Ellie as if he were seeing her for the first time. "Say, how old are you, lassie?"

Ellie hesitated, wishing to disclose no further information to this crude and inquisitive stranger. But she dare not upset him. "I'm . . . twenty-one."

"You ain't married, are you?"

Ellie blushed. "N-no, sir."

"But I see by your color that you wish to be!" Mr. Greaves slapped his knee and guffawed. "Now won't Jed like that!"

"Pardon?"

"Jed is mine and Bonny's first boy. He's keen on girls. He wants to move here with us, but Mazie ain't much in favor of his follerin' us. She says he'll just make trouble.

But what kid don't? And seeing as Bonny can't handle the boy—he don't hold a lick of respect for the hired man—I guess I'll be obliged to haul him along wherever I move. He'll sure want to come here when I tell him what sort of girls grow in these woods."

"I'm sorry, sir, but he would not find me companionable, I'm afraid, since I . . ."

"Since what?"

"I'm . . . spoken for."

"That wouldn't make no matter to Jed!" His dirty moustache twitched. "I don't see no horse and no conveyance, so I calculate that you live nearby. Am I right?"

Ellie tried to refocus the conversation, shifting it away from herself. "Sir, this house is not for sale or rent, I'm sure. I know of no farms in this area that could be bought. Most of us homesteaded here and will be here on our land until we die."

"I like it." He clapped his hamlike hands together with a crack that made Ellie jump. "A stable area. Stable people. Good neighbors. I thank you for the information, miss. I'll be sure to check and see what I can do. I'm sure we will enjoy neighboring here near you. The land man will know the laws."

With an exaggerated bow, the man was gone. Ellie stared down at the muddy spot where he had stood, wondering if she had really seen anyone or if her befuddled mind might be playing tricks on her. And if he were not a figment of her imagination, what had he meant by his departing words? *We will enjoy neighboring here near you.* How dare anyone to try to take over the Brock home place while they were away! It would be nothing short of theft!

Anger and fear boiled together in the caldron of her

emotions. She waited to be sure that the despicable man was gone; then she got up and paced the floor to calm her racing pulse. The letter crackled at her breast.

Ah, yes! The letter! She tore at the envelope with palpitating heart. For five years she'd waited for some word...

"My darling Ellie." It was Daniel's own handwriting —tangible, beautiful. She had to clear her eyes of blinding tears before she could go on reading. She could almost hear Daniel's voice speaking the words. "The hardest thing I've ever done is to leave you without seeing you and telling you goodbye today. But since you are in school and I haven't time to come to you, this hurried note must suffice."

Ellie remembered that day in school. Three times the schoolmarm scolded her for her lack of attention. But how could she concentrate on the slate board when all she could see when she closed her eyes was a heart-shaped cut on the tree with Daniel's initials and hers? What good was elocution and geography and arithmetic, she had thought at the time, when she planned to marry and raise babies and cook blackberry pie?

She read on. "At the next meeting at our tree, I had planned to tell you about my family's plans to travel west with the wagons. I put it off as long as I could, hoping that Paw would change his mind and we wouldn't go after all. But today the man came for us, ahead of schedule and in a hurry to be on the trail. Paw has kept me busy.

"I must go with my family, of course, because I am not of age. But I shall return for you when I reach manhood. Two years seems a very long time, my darling, but I feel like Jacob in the Bible. It will seem but a short while

for the love I have in my heart for you."
Two years. No, two years wouldn't have been so long. Daniel would have returned about the time of her mother's death. He could have supported her in her grief, helped her through the black valley of death. Why didn't he return? More tears came to distort the words that marched like gallant soldiers across the page.

"You need never worry that I will find someone to take your place in my heart while I am away. Go back to *our* tree when you are lonely. Let the wooden heart tell you of my love again. Unless disaster claims me, I will be with you in two years."

Unless disaster claims me. The sentence sent a piercing pain through Ellie. She hadn't thought of this. Many didn't make it across the desert. Stories drifted back from caravans—stories of murders, death from starvation or thirst, Indian raids. . . . This new possibility squeezed at her throat until she could not swallow. *He has met with disaster.*

"Pray for me, beloved, as I pray for you." This was his closing remark, carefully written and underlined.

There! He was praying. God would not allow a tragedy to separate them forever. She could not—would not—believe that Daniel was dead. He *would* return for her!

The letter was signed with a hasty closing and a heart that circled his initials and hers. Why it had been dropped and never reached her was but one of the many unanswered questions that outran answers.

With a puddle of tears still on her cheeks, she slid the letter back into her dress against her breast and started for home. Her blood ran sluggish and cold now. An icy, sickening sensation numbed her.

Three years . . . four years . . . five years . . .
Oh, Daniel, what has happened that has kept you from fulfilling your promise to come back to me?

CHAPTER FOUR
New Neighbors

*E*llie's hands worked, sometimes pottering at meaningless tasks. But her heart seemed dead, turned to stone.

She did not return to her trysting place for fear of meeting Mr. Greaves again. And with this one bright thread in her woof of drab existence gone, she supposed, weary thought, that she would finish out her monotonous days here on her father's farm in the timeworn pattern of day and night, sleeping and waking, winter and summer —and the dreaded trips to the well for water. Stuck in a muddy backwash with no movement or change, she would watch the current of life pass her by. One by one, her brothers would marry and leave, and she would be left, a hopeless spinster, to care for her aging father. *All I'll ever have will be the wooden heart on the tree....*

Five school days, then Saturday and Sunday. Each week was exactly the same as the one before. Lunches and washing and ironing and mending. The only addition to this ritual was her father's frequent "business trips." They had woven themselves smoothly into the week's pattern now.

There was something unusual about Mr. Webster's trips to Springdale. He always wore the black suit, his sleeve garters, and his suspenders. Once Ellie thought she caught a scent of spice as he passed by. Later, she discovered that one of her spice bags was missing. He must have had it in his pocket. But why? What would he need spice for? What it all meant she did not know. Nor had she the energy or the care to take the wrappings off her father's mysterious actions so that she might see them better.

She did notice, however, that the more attention he gave to preparing for these all-day outings, the less attention he gave his sons. And once when young Willy asked to skip a day of school to go with his father, he was strictly forbidden the pleasure. Mr. Webster's voice was sharp when he gave the negative answer.

"Some new folks moved in over at th' Brock place, Paw," Ellie heard Travis, with a mouth not quite emptied of biscuit, tell his father one morning at breakfast.

"Bought it?"

"I'm thinkin' so."

"I didn't know it was for sale."

"Can't locate th' owners. Th' land man said they could live there fer now since those who left it had been gone so long. And if no one comes back to claim it in a certain time of them livin' there, they can file papers to get it for their own, permanent, see. That is, if the records show no one has paid th' taxes. That's th' same as buying it."

"Oh, I expect the Brocks will some day be back, Travis. Some of the kids will show up, anyhow."

Ellie found stirring to do at the cookstove so that her back could betray no emotion to her family. The heart she thought lifeless beneath her ribs leaped. What if the Brock family hadn't paid taxes in all these years? What had the slovenly man with muddy boots said? After a certain time, would some state laws give the land to inquirers who would pay the delinquent taxes? She splashed some gravy onto the stove and it hissed; she had not made quite enough the first time, and her father had scolded her. He was harder to please every day.

"Has th' family got any kids?" This from thirteen-year-old Willy.

"A bunch. But most of them ain't moved here . . . or somethin'. They hail from a long piece off."

"How do you know so much?" Jimmy reached for the butter dish.

"Heard th' talk at school."

"Any my age?" Willy asked.

"Bound to be one or two."

"Now wait, boys," barked Mr. Webster. "We'll want to see what sort of reputation these folks earn before we get thick as jersey cream with them. Birds of a feather flock together, and I'll need to know if I can approve of any flocking."

"It'd be hard to spurn a next-over neighbor," reminded Jimmy. "I hope there's one my age."

"Have they got *girls?*" Willy grimaced.

"Only a little 'un with them," Travis reported. "But they got a growed-up boy 'bout ripe for marryin'. That might interest somebody around here."

Ellie felt the stares of the whole clan puncture her back, but she stirred the faster, splashing more gravy onto the lid of the protesting black stove.

"You're sure spilling today, Ellie," pointed out Mr.

Webster. When she made no reply, he turned back to the boys. "What is the name of this new family?" he asked.

"Greaves. Th' big boy's name is Jed."

"Have you seen him, Travis?" Jimmy quizzed.

"Handsome brute."

"What makes you so slow with the second pan of gravy this mornin', Ellie?" complained Walter, the youngest Webster, sitting on the brink of his eleventh year. "My plate's tired of waitin'. We're hungry men at this here table."

"You forgot to say grace." When Ellie turned, her face was a flushed glower of confusion. Indignation that Mr. Greaves would take over the Brock property mingled with Travis's hint of a suitor for her had left her weak. Her head throbbed with the pressure of racing blood. She gritted her teeth to stop their nervous chattering.

When breakfast passed into history, the menfolk scattered. Ellie grabbed up the water bucket and ran toward the well, glad to be away from the room that might still hold echoes of the contemptible conversation. For some time now, her family had been casting not-so-subtle hints that she should be thinking of bringing in a husband for herself. Until lately, it had just been her brothers who taunted her. Now her father had joined the conspiracy. Oh, they would want her close by, to be sure. At least until one of them chose a wife to take her place in the kitchen. Pharaoh-like, they would expect as many "bricks" from her, leaving her with her own straw to gather. Well, they could forget it. She was not marrying any "handsome brute." The epitaph of her one and only love was carved on a tree.

The outrage of her wounded spirit overshadowed

memory as she sped by the tree with its heart-shaped reminder. The bucket swung back and forth sharply, venting its grating complaint. For strangers to take Daniel's land was to take from Ellie her last straw of hope that he would return to claim it—and her. *Five years is a very long time.* The voice came from within her. *Daniel is either dead . . . or married to someone else.* Doggedly, she shoved the bitter thoughts away with a half sob.

A bird scolded. The evening sun, shining through the dying leaves, cast lacy images all around Ellie. It was unseasonably warm for October. Maroon leaves, clinging past their appointed lifespan, seemed reluctant to yield themselves to the waiting earth. Or were they held by the grasp of the mother tree dreading the bareness of winter?

Absorbed in the brown study of an aimless future without Daniel, Ellie neither saw nor heard the young man who watched her with his careless eyes as she pulled the rope that hoisted the filled cylinder from the depths of the well, bringing cold water. She gave a startled cry at finding him beside her.

"Oh, I see that you're the squeamish kind, pet," he said without preamble. His voice reminded her of a keen lash. "I don't hurt lassies with beautiful buckskin-colored hair, though I've always wanted to see one close up. Buckskins are rare, you know." He imposed his nearness, and Ellie stiffened, starting to back away.

"We might as well get acquainted, since we're neighbors now," he prattled on, ignoring her lack of interest. "I'm Jed Greaves. You must be the lassie my father was telling me about. My, but they do grow nice buckskins in this neck of the woods!"

Ellie kept backing up, afraid to take her eyes from the willful young man lest she miss the intent of his scarred soul. A nameless shame sent hot waves up her neck as his wanton gaze roved over her body.

"Your brother said we could borrow from your well until we get the rubbish cleared out of our own. It hasn't been used in years now, and it needs a good clearing. Say, but I'm going to like our new place! Especially with a bonnie thing like you close by. Travis told me he had a sister. But he didn't tell the half what my eyes tell me. But then, one can't very well explain in color. Not a pretty buckskin color, anyway. Well, well, what a streak of good luck! . . ."

Ellie felt a flame rise high on each cheekbone. She hit him with her cold stare. If he had come for water, where was his container?

"What's your name?" he persisted.

Ellie didn't answer.

"Cat got your tongue?"

Trussing up her skirt and darting away like a scared chaparral, Ellie left Jed and her water bucket sitting on the lip of the well as she raced toward the house. He reminded her somehow of a hungry wolf. The ravenous inventory his eyes had taken of her made her skin prickle.

He was strikingly handsome, she had to admit, with his unruly, dark hair and brash, black eyes. But those eyes were not true; his lips curled with contempt. Ellie wanted nothing to do with him. Only when she was sure that he had gone did she return for her bucket.

Now she had yet another reason for dreading the daily fetching of water. The memory of her last day with Daniel was trial enough, but now a fear, that she might again meet the awful young man there, sat down on the bench with memory, and the two, posing side by side in Ellie's mind, made her heart weak with trepidation.

The brothers brought Ellie's name into their conversation again at the timber sawing. Their talk followed the same map as it had before.

"Did Ellie ask you to start bringin' up th' water from th' well for her?" Jimmy straightened and look directly at Travis.

"She did. But I ain't. An' you ain't neither. I just dare you to do it for her."

"Why, Travis? I sorta feel sorry for her. We're boys, an' we're a lot stronger than she is."

"Listen, Jimmy. You don't know the first thing about women. If you start cottonin' to 'em and doin' things to favor 'em, they start to get weak on you. It might start with just fetchin' water, but next thing you know, she'd want you to do somethin' else. It never stops with just one thing. There's always another."

"Like next she'd want us to milk th' cows?"

"Yep. Then gather eggs. You get th' idea, chap. We can't cotton to Ellie just 'cause she don't like goin' to th' well. She's got her work an' we got ours. We wouldn't 'spect her to chop wood or push an' pull this crosscut saw to hew down th' tree, now would we? An' remember this: we got school an' she don't."

"Yeah, school."

"Don't ever let yourself get trapped into startin' to feel sorry for a woman, Jimmy. Any woman. They thrive on pity. Then it turns to self-pity. An' a self-pityin' woman's worse than a half-broke bronc. They ain't good for a thing."

"I believe, though, that if we'd do that one little chore

for Ellie she'd ask no more."

"You may be right, an' you may not. But we can't take no chances. We ain't goin' to cut her no slack. We can't have her goin' soft on us. She might just decide some mornin' not to even get up an' cook our mush! Now wouldn't that be a pretty come-off? How would you like to pack your own lunch while she queened around sickly-like? Anyways, it wouldn't be no favor to th' husband she marries for us, her own brothers, to start spoilin' her now! Who wants a spoiled-rotten wife?"

"I don't believe she's ever goin' to wed, nohow."

"Ellie never marry?"

"Oh, it ain't 'cause she ain't pretty, or hard workin', or of marryin' age. She just don't seem . . . interested in marryin'."

"You've forgot, Jimmy, that we have a new marryin'-age neighbor that's mighty easy on th' eyes to look at! An' looks count a lot with girls. He's got a wily way about him, too. She'll be sparkin' him afore spring sprouts in these hills."

"I'm thinkin' not."

CHAPTER FIVE

The Drifter

"*I* hired on a drifter to help out with the livestock through the winter, Ellie." Mr. Webster held his tin cup suspended in midair, an unspoken command for her to refill it with cold buttermilk. "I don't have as much time on my hands as I used to—what with all these trips I must make into town every week." He gave a nervous half cough. "And my rheumatiz is bothering me worse this year, too. The new hand will be coming out next week. I met him in Springdale, and he said he was strong enough to give a man a week's work in one day."

"You have four healthy boys to share the work, Father," objected Ellie. The thoughts of an outsider in the home, and male at that, agitated her.

"The boys beg off work for their schooling," Mr. Webster said. "It's important for a lad to get his education nowadays. It isn't like it used to be when I was a boy. We live in modern times, and it takes book learning to get anywhere in the world. Why, they're even talking about a horseless carriage!"

"A *horseless* carriage?"

"Yes. It's a contraption run by machine instead of pulled by a horse. They'll do it. You wait and see. And it'll be in our day—mine and yours."

Ellie was sure her brothers used school as an excuse to get out of chores. She noticed that the duty they sought to escape hid behind the skirts of "lessons." Their fondness of school was nothing more than a fondness of hours away from the confining farm and its never-ending work, and their grades reflected their indifference.

Ellie frowned. "Mayhap, Paw, if you'd cut down on your trips to town. . . ."

"No need to worry about the cowboy I hired on, Ellie. He won't give any problems. He's all shut up in himself and don't have much to say to nobody. I've never found hired help at such a bargain. He agreed to come just for a place to sleep, his food, and some small change for life's little necessities. I threw a horse into the deal. I wouldn't want to take advantage of a fellow's goodness. He hasn't got no family and scarce more than the clothes on his back, poor soul. He said I could let him go anytime he became a burden instead of a blessing.

"I take it he doesn't know the first thing about farming and timber, but he said he was a fast and willing learner. He does know a lot about livestock. He's used to roaming, so I expect I'll do good to hold him the winter. And mayhap he won't even show up for work."

I'll pray that he doesn't, Ellie promised herself.

But the cowboy that Mr. Webster employed came. He made his bed in the hayloft and only came to the house for his meals, which he ate in polite silence. He may as well have been a post or a chair or a wall peg for all the attention he gave anyone or anyone gave him. For the most part, Ellie forgot he was seated at the family table. One more to cook for bothered her but little. A woman's hands were made for labor, and her fingers found their way among crocks and iron skillets while her mind lived in the abstraction of bygone days with Daniel. Cups and plates went onto the oilcloth-covered harvest table by rote.

Wayne—that is what Ellie heard the boys call the newcomer—was certainly nothing to look upon. Ellie found herself comparing him to an upright skeleton with scant pads of flesh added here and there to fill in the vacant spots.

He appeared gaunt and underfed, and it seemed to her that he ate very little in comparison to her own robust brothers. But he was tall, broad of shoulder, and sinewy. He may even have been pleasing to the eye in better days. Now, though, one bad eye and ragged scars on his face sabotaged any good looks he may have once had. An ear had suffered some sort of chewing. His speech, a short thanks for the meal each day, was slurred from a mouth of injury. He seemed self-conscious and shy, especially when Ellie filled his cup.

"He's the best worker I ever had," Mr. Webster boasted. "And the cheapest. I hope he'll stay the winter—or at least until my business in Springdale is sewed up."

As the weeks passed, the only resentment Ellie could find to carry in her bosom toward the drifter was that another man washing his hands at the speckled, granite wash basin before meals necessitated more trips to the well for water. This called for setting her face as a flint and accomplishing the task as quickly as possible. She told herself that she had rather take a beating than go for water. Yet she knew that if the man realized he was causing her any anguish, he would put his hand-cleansing manners aside and never utilize her precious commodity. She felt badly for begrudging him this luxury.

The new man didn't try to make small talk or take any notice of her; this was a relief to Ellie. The single "Thank you" for the meal was his sole acknowledgement of her presence. So, really, nothing would change because he came to work for her father, she decided.

But things did change. Slowly and imperceptibly the change came. One morning when rain spat at the windows and the air threatened a cold norther, Ellie opened the back door and found the woodbox beside the stoop filled with kindling and twigs. Stacked neatly nearby was a day's supply of wood for the cookstove as well as the pot-bellied heater in the day room. Travis had never been so thoughtful, and Ellie stared at the wood with open surprise. She was pleased that her brother showed such forethought and concern for her. It was a good sign, something she wished her mother could know. She would be proud of the man Travis was becoming.

When Travis came blustering in for his rawhide work gloves, she stopped him with a smile of sisterly gratitude. "It was mighty kind of you to fetch up the wood for me, Travis," she said. "I appreciate that."

Travis gave her a curious, blank look. "I didn't bring up no wood for you," he said. "You're thankin' th' wrong person." Then he scuttled out the door and was gone.

It must have been Jimmy that did the good turn for her, Ellie decided. But when she tried to thank the next oldest of the boys, he waved away her words of appreciation.

"Don't thank me. Sure wadn't me what did it, Ellie." He shrugged. "Mighty thoughty of whoever did, though."

After expressing gratefulness to all four boys and receiving the same shocked reaction from each of them, Ellie was perplexed. Could it have been her father who brought the wood from the shed in her stead? No. To Mr. Webster, chores were chores, and he never infringed on assigned work except in dire illness. On this score, he was unrelenting.

There was only one other person who could have done the favor for her. That was Wayne, the cowhand. But why should he have bothered? He didn't even stay in the house to enjoy the results of his labors. His wages were poor; why should he volunteer to do more than his necessary work?

The next day a cold wind sliced through the shedding trees. Ellie bundled up in warm clothing to milk the cows. However, when she stepped out to the lean-to screened porch, two buckets of warm, steaming milk sat just inside the door ready to be strained and bottled. Her brothers had never milked a cow in their lives; they probably wouldn't know how. And her father was away on his "business trip." There was no question as to who put the milk there.

As the days crawled by, bringing longer nights and bitter weather, other little courtesies showed up, lightening Ellie's workload. She hardly knew what to make of it and almost resented the extra hours it gave her, hours to fight away despair and loneliness. To fill the lagging hours, she cross-stitched a plaque of the Ten Commandments.

The trips to the well were no less painful. On her way

there early one frost-bitten morning, Ellie heard the clear ring of an axe on wood. A pale and reluctant sun offered scant warmth to her body, allowing it to become as cold as her heart. She felt that she could not bear to pass the memorable tree today—her tree and Daniel's—and could not relive the day of their lost love one more time. She had dreamed of him during the previous chilly night and awoke in a fog of depression. Except for the others who depended on her, she would gladly have left the bucket empty and suffered thirst, thus avoiding the dread journey that took her by the heart-shaped carving.

Through the brushy woods, thinned of its foliage now by winter's approach, she saw the movement of Wayne's gangling arms as they lifted the handle of the axe for a crushing blow. Something within her bolted, and she dropped her bucket and lurched forward, crazed with a horrible thought. He might unwittingly cut down the wrong tree for firewood! He might cut down *her* tree. Panic made her wild.

"Wait!" she screamed, her violet eyes saucer-shaped and begging. "Don't cut down *that* tree!"

He stood with the axe poised beside the tree—her tree and Daniel's. At the sound of her frantic call, he dropped the axe and looked to her for an explanation of her irrational behavior.

"Oh, sir! Please don't cut *that* tree down," she beseeched earnestly, the tears coming unbidden. "That's . . . my special tree. Any of the other trees on the place will be all right for firewood, but I can't . . . stand to see that one felled. Please!"

He might think her insane—and she might well be. But she cared not what he, or anyone, thought. The tree belonged to her and Daniel. It was all they had as joint property. This last memory held the fragments of her broken dream. And if her dream was taken from her, she would fall to her death with the tree.

"I'm . . . I'm sorry, miss." Without another word or a glance toward Ellie, the man found a dried sapling nearby and began to chop it into lengths of logs.

Ellie's lips trembled. Her hands shook. Her legs wobbled. The thoughts of how closely she had come to losing her tree took away her strength. How could she get her filled bucket back to the house?

When she returned from the well, stopping every few steps to rest, the hired man dropped his tool and took her burden in spite of her objections. She ran on ahead, not wishing to walk along with him, tears falling inside now and threatening to drown her heart.

She had saved her tree. But what if she had not gone for water just when she did? She clenched her teeth at the unbearable thought.

The man set the filled bucket on the washstand, an unpainted table weathered to a sickly gray, and turned to leave without meeting Ellie's eyes.

CHAPTER SIX

Trouble at the Well

Jimmy splashed water from the tin foot tub onto his face, generously applying the nondescript-shape cake of lye soap to his tawny skin.

"The Greaves finally got their well cleaned out," he reported, burying his face in a rough towel.

"I didn't mind sharing them our water. But it will be more convenient for them, and much closer, to get water from their own well again," Mr. Webster said.

"They sure like the Brock place. They're going to get it changed over to their name legally as soon as they can. I guess they're here for good."

"They seem like peaceable neighbors. One of our cows got over into their field. Even helped herself to their haystack. And Mr. Greaves just laughed about it. That's the kind of next-overs I like. Folk that won't ruffle the waters over every little wave-splashing pebble. It grieved me to lose the Brocks. They were as fine a folk as the world holds. We'll never find better neighbors. But it looks like they don't plan on coming back."

Travis turned to Ellie. "Have you been over to meet the new neighbor lady, Ellie?"

Ellie pulled the cornpone from the warming oven and almost dropped it. "No, I haven't."

"She's right young looking. She might like some woman company, being new here and all."

Ellie said nothing. She would find no pleasure in making friends with the wife of a land stealer. Mr. Greaves planned to take the Brocks' farm without their permission. She wanted nothing to do with thieves.

"Yes, Ellie. You might bake a berry pie and take over to show yourself neighborly," suggested her father. "That's what your maw would have done."

Learning that the neighboring well supplied good water again, Ellie dropped her fear of meeting Jed, the fear that had turned each trip for water into a living nightmare in spite of her careful surveillance. Now only the nagging memory of Daniel nipped at the heels of her mind as her feet dragged down the miserable path. The fear had been a torment; the memory was a bittersweet pain.

So when Jed appeared quite unexpectedly in the evening shadows while Ellie concentrated on the rope and the pulley, she almost dropped her bucket into the well in her dismay. The even white teeth bared by his ruthless smile might have been fangs in the illusion of Ellie's fright. Icy fingers of panic tore at her throat, threatening to still even her breath.

"I can't understand why you're so skittish, kitten." Jed smiled his slyest. "You're not very tame, are you? Haven't been around civilization, I presume. Ah, but we can fix that. I've tamed a lot of kittens before. It's a hobby of mine. A few parties, a few dances, a few drinks.

A trip to the city. Then you'll learn to purr like the next."

Ellie started to run, but Jed put out his foot, and she tripped over it. Before she fell, he reached for her arm and set her back upright with a smirk of pleased satisfaction.

"Not so quick there, pet. We need to have a little talk. I might as well start in to domesticate you right away. There's no call for you to be such a wild little thing. I know you do have a tongue. And since your brothers speak English, I would guess that you do, too. I don't spend my energy on just any idle project. But you're not a bad looker. That buckskin hair fascinates me."

"You . . . don't even . . . know me." Ellie shuddered, trying to keep the tremor invisible. *He must not know how frightened I am.*

A shadow caricature that stretched across the well, sketched by the falling rays of a watery sun, sent Ellie into spasms of terror as it bent and crooked to conform to the shapeless stones. She didn't trust this loose-tongued man by day, much less in the gathering darkness. She looked about frantically, seeking escape.

"Why, you can talk, can't you?" Mockery and scorn met in his cold eyes. "And I probably know a great deal more about you than you realize. I've been doing a bit of sleuthing. You can make heavenly baking-powder explosions and red-eye gravy and the best berry pie this side of Eden. You can cross-stitch and knit and darn socks. That's an asset. You get a good grade there. But you're religious to a fault and make your brothers say blessings at the table; that's a strike against you. And you're old enough to think about being my wife. So you may as well get to thinking."

"I'll . . . *never* marry you."

"There you go again. With your back arched and hissing like a barnyard kitten at a stick. Don't bite off the hand that's trying to feed you, kitty. I'll provide quite well for you. My old man will get restless and move on in a few months, and this property we're getting the deed to will be mine. And yours, kitty."

Ellie loathed the child-placating tones he used as he spoke and the haughty pride that disgraced his swarthy face.

"If you'll excuse me now . . . " Ellie moved to retrieve her bucket and make her getaway.

"No, I won't excuse you, pet. Not yet. You'll pay me the respect of waiting until I'm through talking to you before you leave."

"I'll . . . never respect a . . . beast like you. Respect can't be demanded. It has to be earned."

"Oh, we have a philosopher here! Well, kitten, I'll pluck your own word-weapons from your hands and use them on you so you can see how they feel: You don't even know me!" Jed threw back his head in a gelid laugh. "But you shall, of course."

"I won't marry anyone except . . . except Daniel," she blurted indignantly, with a determined lift of her quivering chin. "I could never love anyone else."

"And who is this Daniel? Some guy who was pitched into a den of lions?"

Ellie set her lips, spurning his impudence.

"I asked, who is Daniel?" he repeated, his voice more demanding this time. The contest of wills pleased Jed, inciting his evil nature.

"Daniel is the son of the man whose land you stole!

Thieves, that's what you people are! Daniel's father didn't say that you could have their land and their house and their . . ."

Angered, Jed grabbed her arm roughly, squeezing it with the pressure of his awkward hand. "Ah, now I'm getting the picture. My old man told me he found you sitting in the house mooning at the ceiling like a sick calf. He said that you were obsessed with the place and had been pawing around in the dirt outside. So the place belonged to *Daaaaniel.*" He stretched out the name and then spat it with venom, jealousy blazing in his eyes. He shook her. "Look here. I didn't steal anybody's land. If this Daniel wants his land, or his lassie, he'd better show up to claim them mighty quick. Because I intend to have *both.*"

The trees began to swim in a crazy, illusionary pattern. Ellie's breath came short, and she felt herself sliding down. A merciful blackness swallowed her. She crumbled to the ground in a pitiful little senseless heap.

Jed, consumed by black fury, failed to see Mr. Webster's hired man hurl himself like a volcanic eruption from behind a blind of brush beyond the well. He tried to leap away from the strong farmhand, but Wayne clamped his powerful fingers like a vise on Jed's bony shoulder and held him.

"What happened to the lady?" Wayne demanded.

"I'm sure I don't . . . know, sir. I was just trying to . . . to help her fill her bucket there with water . . . uh, doing a good deed, . . . and she just . . . she just up and went into a faint." He gave a sawed-off laugh. "You know how delicate women folks are." His dark-brown eyes held cowardice.

"Did you say something to upset her?" Wayne's jaw muscles bunched.

"Oh, no, sir! Nothing at all. No, I'm sure that nothing I said could possibly have upset her. I just . . . asked her if I might help . . . like any gentleman would do for a lady . . . who . . . who . . . needed help with her water bucket."

"It happens that not everything you said to the lady slighted my ears, Jed Greaves. I don't appreciate a liar *or* a thief."

"Why, I'm . . . I'm neither."

"Didn't I just hear the lady say that you were taking over land that belongs to someone else?"

"The lady doesn't understand, Mr.—Mr.—"

"My name is Wayne."

"Mr. Wayne. Legally, it's . . ."

"What I want to know is if it's morally right for you to take another man's land."

"We're . . . uh . . . just planning to *rent* the land, I believe, sir. The money will go into a trust fund for the owners . . . uh . . . should they decide to return in the future. That's fair enough, isn't it?"

"You're trying my temperance to the limit. If I didn't have at least a smattering of the religion you scorned the girl for having, I would turn you to sausage."

Jed Greaves licked his dry lips.

"But I am a Christian, and I believe in giving a man a chance. The best thing for you to do in the future is to stay off Mr. Webster's property altogether and not set foot on the place unless you are personally invited. If the lady wants you, she'll send for you, and I'll be the last one to raise objections to her wishes. Until then . . ."

Jed turned to hurry away, but Wayne blocked his exit.

"You'd leave the lady lying on the wet ground to catch her death of cold? Jed, you're a worse shade of yellow than I imagined." Wayne's scalding look was designed to burn into Jed's soul.

But Jed still tried to sneak away, seeking nothing but a hasty departure for himself, safe from Wayne's reach.

Wayne stepped aside. "Go on, Jed. And be quick about it! I'll take care of the lady. I wouldn't trust a rat like you to touch her. She's too pure for your vile hands!"

He waved Jed on his way and gathered the limp girl into his hard-muscled arms. She was so lovely and feathery light that he swallowed twice to clear the choking sensation in his throat. To think that anyone who called himself a man would hurt or frighten a fragile thing like this!

Unfortunately, Wayne had heard part of the conversation by the well. He had heard this lovely girl say that she could never love another.

When Ellie awoke, she was on her own bed with a damp compress against her forehead. A tall figure stood in the doorway and then disappeared as her eyes began to focus. Who could it be? It was all a bad dream, of course.

CHAPTER SEVEN
Mr. Webster's Surprise

"Fix up a special supper tonight, Ellie. I'm bringing a guest to eat with us," Mr. Webster said before he left for town at daybreak. "Be sure to make one of your famous berry pies."

"But I have only one jar of berries left, Father," she objected. "And I was saving that for Christmas."

"I want the pie today." He held his chin high, and Ellie got a whiff of the spice again. The dread of an unknown happening grappled at her sluggish sixth sense.

Now she stood on the braided doormat looking over the bleak front yard, her eyes glued on the rutted road beyond. Her nerves were pulled taut, tied in a knot of tension. An old tree near the house shadowed the hour; her father should be arriving anytime now. It was so unlike him to invite a guest to their home.

For no reason in particular, she sighed. The ham was glazed and the berry pie a picture-perfect shade of amber. It might have graced the cover of a farm journal. She was, she admitted to herself without the germ of pride, a good cook if nothing else.

Whoever this gentleman was that Mr. Webster had invited for supper must be an important businessman. She wondered if her father might be negotiating with someone to sell the home place.

Why the negotiations should require so many appointments was beyond her. Mr. Webster actually neglected the home-front duties.

Except for leaving behind the tree with the heart-shaped carving on it, she would be glad to move away so that she would never have to lay eyes on Jed Greaves again. A chill passed through her body, but not from the cold. Her mind somersaulted back to the day that Jed accosted her at the well when she went for water. Something had seemed to turn brown around the edges in her soul, scorched by his vulgar words.

How she got home from the well with her water bucket she could not remember. She supposed that she had managed to stumble to her room in some sort of stupor. Perhaps she was even losing her mind. No one had mentioned the incident, and if her father or her brothers had come for her, they would have broadcast the fact and taunted her for her ridiculous fear of a "harmless neighbor."

Certainly she had drained the cup of sorrow to its dregs, and there could be no greater pain for her to endure. There had been the loss of Daniel, and her mother's death—now the devil himself had moved in for a neighbor!

She felt that she would never be able to return to the well even if it meant that her whole family died of thirst. Her legs simply would not take her there. But that problem had been mercifully solved. Since the encounter with

Jed three days before, the bucket had been refilled by someone before its water level fell below the halfway mark. Ellie didn't know who to thank for this service, for watch as she would, she failed to "catch" the stealthy benefactor. In her heart, though, she knew that the drifter was responsible for the kind deed.

The relief would be temporary at best. Mr. Webster had only hired the man for the winter months. Then he would move on. What would Ellie do when he was gone?

She heard the squawk of ungreased wheels before she saw the silhouette of her father's buggy come into view against the faded December sky. She wondered if the man her father brought would be riding his own horse, but she soon saw that no horse followed. Apparently, the visitor rode in the vehicle with her father.

Would the guest spend the night? There was no place but the attic for him to sleep. No, she rationalized, it would not be proper to lodge a businessman, a prospective buyer of their property, in the unheated loft. She would be obliged to give him her room and make a pallet in the pantry for herself. She hoped her father had considered the limitations of their household. They were not as well-heeled as the moneyed gentleman going through the country buying up land.

As the buggy neared, Ellie strained her eyes to see. A bundled-up figure hunched near her father. The man must be ill or very old. Finances had been tight all summer, she knew, but would her father resort to some irrational arrangement such as taking in a boarder for the sake of money? If so, this posed yet another problem. How could she give nursing care to a sick man while trying to feed and care for six healthy and active ones?

Mr. Webster lifted his guest to the ground, and they were almost to the door before Ellie realized that the visitor wasn't a man at all—she was a woman! What . . . ?

"Ellie, this is your new maw." Mr. Webster's words were close-cropped and pointed. "We were married today in Springdale."

The door facing moved closer to Ellie's face and then backed off as she swayed with the shock of her father's words. Surely she hadn't heard it! He didn't mean it! *Married?* Her father? No!

"Do . . . the boys know?"

"Nobody knows!" Her father gave a snort of laughter. "I wanted to surprise all of you. And I see that I did." He favored the woman at his side with a playful wink. "Mrs. Webster, this is your new daughter, Ellie."

"The one who makes the *delightful* berry pies, Ronald?" Her voice was affected, stagy. "I'm pleased to meet you, my dear," she said to Ellie. "You do favor your handsome father! And I can hardly wait to taste your delicious cookery!"

Ellie's glance touched the pudgy woman. The last thing this pudding-faced dame needed, she thought, was another helping of dessert.

"Why, Ellie made a pie just for you, my sweetie," Ellie heard her father saying. She wanted to stop her ears and run from the room. She did *not* make the pie for an unwanted stepmother! "We'll eat right away, and then you two will have a chance to become better aquainted."

"Yes, by all means. Let's eat *first*. I am famished," the woman crooned. "Then we'll make some family plans for the future of all of us."

The boys gathered at Mr. Webster's shrill whistle.

They passed awkward side glances between themselves when their father broke the news of his wedding and introduced his bride. Wayne nodded stiffly, and Ellie found her eyes searching his face for his reaction to the sudden announcement. He seemed solicitous and sympathetic. She hid her emotions behind a mask of indifference, asumed at a great cost.

Supper was a stilted, silent meal except for the new Mrs. Webster's constant prattle. Mr. Webster seemed not to notice—or to care. He had eyes only for his new wife and gave avid attention to each idle, empty word that she spoke.

A cobweb of habit kept Ellie's hands and feet going during the serving of the meal, her father's wedding feast. She ate little herself; the food that looked so good an hour ago now stuck in her throat in lumps that could not be swallowed. Her mind churned, the dasher of her reasoning plunging up and down, trying desperately to bring some solid order to the chaos that fermented within her spirit. Did her father actually expect her to accept this gregarious woman as a replacement of her own dear, quiet, little mother? Would this garish outsider become their mentor, their example, their guide?

After a generous helping of pie, the talkative lady suggested that she and Mr. Webster look about the place while Ellie cleared the table. Caught in a tidal wave of emotional crosscurrents, Ellie closed her eyes and whispered a prayer for grace. *And I thought nothing worse could happen!* It seemed to her that as soon as she chopped down one problem, another grew in its place.

From the next room, hushed comments reached Ellie's ears. "She'll never be *my* mother!" spat Walter. "I won't mind a thing she says."

"Did you see the beet juice she has on her cheeks and on her lips? *My* mother would never stain her face with beet juice! What did Paw see in that old bag?" This was Willy's voice.

"She's lazy, or she'd be in there helping Ellie with the dishes."

"Where will she sleep? Paw's cot ain't big enough for 'um both."

"What's her name? Where did Paw find her?"

"I heard Paw call her Bea. Isn't that a dumb name for a growed-up woman? Now we know what all those business trips was about. Business, me eye!"

Ellie felt her brothers' complaints, and even their disrespect, to be legitimate. Her heart wept for them—four impressionable boys who needed a father so desperately. What would happen if they rebelled, and revolted against their stepmother? She knew in her heart where her father's loyalty would lie: with his new wife. What did the future hold for her, or any of them, now?

Ellie hung a fresh flour-sack towel, bleached and blued to a snowy white, on the wooden towel roller by the wash basin and moved into the sitting room. Her brothers scattered like a covey of quail from a fox when her father and Bea returned from their walk in the yard.

"Bea has a few things she needs to discuss with you, Ellie," her father said in his corner-cutting way. "I'll help the boys stable the horses and put away the buggy while you two settle the inside affairs."

"Sit down, Ellie," commanded the woman, with a wag of her stubby finger. "We might as well start out with a good understanding from the beginning. You and I will have many adjustments to make. We want to make them as painlessly as possible, of course.

"My name is Beatrice. Your father is the only person I will allow to call me Bea. Under no circumstances are you to call me Mother. I'm not the smothery, mothery type. Even my own children never call me that. The very word is frumpy and sentimental. I raised my children to be independent and sophisticated.

"My family and I don't get along too well with each other, so they likely won't be visiting often. When they do visit, though, you are to be extremely courteous and hospitable to them. They faulted me for thinking of marriage so soon after the death of their father. They expected me to dress in a dreadful black garb and keep a lawn handkerchief to dab my tears for a *whole year!* Such an old-fogey idea! I concur with Shakespeare who said let the dead bury the dead, and come and follow me. Now Shakespeare went places in society and in literature. We can afford to sit up and pay attention to the words of a man like that.

"Anyway, as I was saying—what was I saying? Oh, yes. I have two children. A girl and a boy. Both were my husband's absurd idea of happiness. My daughter, Wancille—I like modern names—is divorced from her husband and courts men where she works. She's a soda jerk and very popular. My son is grown, too. His name is Julius, after the famous Caesar. You'll meet my children eventually, but I'm not asking for any family blending. Your family and mine are too diversified. You will feel no more at home around my daughter than she will feel around you. You are . . . well, traditional, and she's not.

"Your father and I agreed from the start to let bygones be bygones. He promised to put out of my sight every reminder of his deceased wife just as I promised to rid myself of the memorials of my first husband. That's as it should be.

"I'll have the larger bedroom here, which I understand from your father is your own. So you will kindly move in with one of your brothers and see that nothing of your mother's is left to annoy me in the room I occupy. Your father wished to bring me to meet his family today. He has promised to take me for my belongings tomorrow. I'm eager to get settled and make the necessary changes for my comfort.

"We'll divide up the work, but you are to understand that I rest each morning. The breakfast and morning chores will be left up to you. I will decide which of the responsibilities will be mine and which will be yours when I have carefully observed your routine here in the country. I am accustomed to city life."

Ellie stared at the toes of her worn shoes, holding a flood of tears with a dike of fierce anger. She could not let this coldhearted, thoughtless woman see her cry!

Beatrice Webster stopped her barrage of talk so abruptly that Ellie looked up to see if she was still there. The woman's coal black hair, fashioned in a modern pompadour and held back with a ridiculous crown-shaped comb, hung low over black-brown eyes that evaluated Ellie.

"I'm glad that you are an agreeable sort," she said after her brief break in the torrent of words. "I was dreadfully afraid you might not be so manageable. I do wish that I might call you Eleanor, though. It sounds so much more dignified than just plain Ellie. Ellie sounds old-fashioned, common. Why it's no wonder that you have never found a beau and gotten married with a name like that! The very idea: twenty-one and still at home with daddy! Well, we'll see to that."

Ellie drew her mouth into a thin line of pain. "I-I don't care to marry, thank you."

Beatrice threw back her head in a merry, mocking laugh. "You are such a little prude. But of course you wish to marry. All young women wish to marry, and you shall!"

"If you'll excuse me. . . ."

"Eleanor, your father tells me that you go overboard with your religious beliefs." Beatrice pointed to the sampler of the Ten Commandments on the wall. "I don't like that." Her voice was edgy. "It's too negative. 'Thou shalt' and 'thou shalt not' . . . It's much too arbitrary. I'm asking that you please remove it; this is my home now."

Ellie snatched the framed cross-stitch pattern from the wall and fled from the room.

CHAPTER EIGHT
The Death of a Dream

*E*llie slept little that night. Events of the day looped and tangled with her dreams; the real and the imaginary fused inseparably into a netherworld nightmare. It was all a bad dream, surely. When she awoke, her eyeballs felt hard and dry and her head pounded.

Mr. Webster came to breakfast without his bride, reporting that she was still asleep. She was subject to headaches, he said, if she was disturbed. They left before lunch in spite of the heavy clouds that banked in the north. Beatrice made no effort to see Ellie before their departure.

Early in the afternoon, a dreadful storm blew in unannounced and dumped sleet and ice on the area, cutting outside comfort to the bone.

"Say, Willy," Walter punched his brother with his elbow and sniggered, "th' woman's trapped out. I'm glad she's trapped *out* 'stead of *in*." Ellie thought she couldn't have said it better. She found immense relief in that thought herself.

It grew colder and colder. The recollection of other winters when chores drove her from the protection of the old house's warmth sent shivers through Ellie's thin frame. But this winter was different. The woodbox replenished itself as if by magic. A basket heaped with brown eggs from the henhouse showed up each morning before breakfast, always in the same place on the side cupboard. Nor did the water bucket ever run low, thanks to the hired hand. But best of all, Ellie was spared the agony of watching her tree battle winter's brutal onslaught, barren and lonely. She felt that this hurt on top of everything else would have crushed her.

The aloof stranger had certainly made her existence less burdensome. But to what advantage? So that she might have idle time to nurse her broken heart? She drew a long, tired breath. How could a dream be so heavy?

Why had she not allowed the man to chop down the tree of sentiment? It symbolized a love that was never to be. She was twenty-one years old and still holding to a teenage fantasy! By and by, a body should grow up, become mature enough to accept life's disappointments.

Travis found Ellie in the kitchen stirring a pot of brown beans. "Ellie, may I invite Wayne to stay up here at the house tonight? It's 'way below freezin' already, an' by nighttime it'll be terrible cold. I'm afraid he might take pneumonia in that drafty old barn."

"Where would he sleep, Travis?"

"In th' attic room. It's cold up there, but not nearly so cold as th' old barn is. Knowin' him, he wouldn't hear to sleepin' down here in th' house with us. He's not th' imposin' kind."

A small request it was—innocent enough—and they all

owed Wayne a great deal. "I . . . suppose it would be all right if you don't think Paw would mind."

"Paw ain't givin' us a thought, Ellie. He's caught up in his own world with that awful woman. And you're to go right back to your room while they are away."

"Oh, no, I—"

"Yes, you will. This storm could last a week or more. We'll have a good time while *she's* gone. We might even make taffy and have a pull. I've got a feelin' our fun times are over when she rules th' roost." He wrinkled his freckle-laden nose. "Us boys wish the storm would last *forever!*"

Wayne brought his bedroll to the house. Almost apologetically, he turned to Ellie: "Your brother insisted I bunk here where it's warmer until the worst of the weather is past. He seemed to be afraid I would take a death of cold."

"It can get bad in this part of the country," Ellie nodded.

"I told Travis I didn't suppose there would be any grieving if I froze to death," he added, not for pity but matter-of-factly.

"Oh, Paw would have a fit," she said. "He'd not find another man to work so hard for him. And I would . . . " She stopped, flustered. "I mean, all these little things you do for me . . . that is, for all of us. . . ." She turned back to the stove, feeling she had made a fool of herself.

After the meal, Ellie busied herself with setting the bread for morning. The boys laughed and talked with Wayne around the pot-bellied stove in the family room. He was comfortable and at home with her brothers. She paid little attention to their conversation at first, but when the discussion turned to some of the people Wayne had met on his travels, she found herself curious.

"Did you ever go to school with anyone by the name of Aaron Brock, Travis? The family was from this area somewhere." In spite of the burr in Wayne's speech, the name came out clearly and Ellie leaned forward. The name jolted her to crystalline attention.

Brock. The man was speaking of Daniel's family? Aaron was Daniel's younger brother. Had he met them on his journeys? Was there a chance he might know of their whereabouts? She held her breath so that she might hear better.

"Yes, they were our neighbors next over," Travis said. "They lived on th' place where th' Greaveses live now. Left here about five year ago for th' run west. Ain't never returned. The land man put a notice in th' paper advertisin' for anyone who knew where they might be. Some legal stuff about their land. I heard Paw talkin' about it. Did you, by any chance, meet up with th' Brocks some place?"

"Yes, I did. Out west in the New Mexico territory in a place the local people call Diablo Pass. They were a family with great plans. They were headed for the California gold mines."

"Paw sure liked the Brocks. They were a fine family, he says. I was just a twelve-year-old kid when they left, but all of us miss 'em yet. You think they'll be comin' back soon? I'm afraid if they don't, they'll lose their land."

"I'm afraid they won't be comin' back at all." His voice was low, and Ellie strained to hear, trying not to miss a word. "They met with . . . bad luck."

Bad luck! Ellie slumped down onto the wooden bench that ran the length of the harvest table. Her head fell against the grease-splattered wall. She wanted to close her ears, lest they hear what they did not wish to hear— what she feared they would hear.

"What sort of bad luck was it?"

"Outlaws. The ruthless kind. The senseless kind. They killed most of the family outright for what few valuables the family had with them. Such needless murders . . . "

"They had a boy named Daniel," Jimmy cut in. "A nice fellow. We—me and Trav—always thought him an' Ellie might strike up a match. She was kind of sweet on him, we thought. I guess she's forgot him by now, though. Never has mentioned his name since th' day they left."

"I knew there was a girl," Wayne's voice held ragged edges. "He mentioned her often."

"Was he killed, too?"

"Trampled by the outlaws' horses, son. It was all so tragic."

Ellie heard no more. When she came to her senses, her throbbing head lay on the table, crutched up by her folded arms. The house was silent. Wearily, she pulled herself to her feet, trying to push away the shocking news that had put her to sleep. With mental fists, she beat away visions of flying hooves. *Oh, please, God, I can't stand the thoughts of Daniel being trampled . . . my Daniel!* She gritted her teeth to keep from crying out loud. Her head felt as though it had been filled with hot liquid.

Her body lurched toward the sitting room. No one was there, and the fire had been banked for the night, a job that usually fell her lot. She checked the damper and found it closed. Then, a prey to black despair, she crept to her bed. Daniel was dead, and she no longer cared whether the next breath found her or not. How could she go on living without her dream?

The sleep her body craved abandoned her, leaving her stranded on the shores of vivid memory. Every word Daniel had spoken, every tender look, came back to haunt her. *Daniel is dead! Daniel is dead!* Tormenting demons screamed at her.

Sometime in the cold, dark night, Ellie heard the sound of a muffled choking sob. She sat up on the edge of her bed, trying to determine which of her brothers might be ill.

The muted sound came from the attic room above, where Wayne had made his bedroll on the floor. She had never heard a grown man cry. Something must be dreadfully wrong! What should she do?

Listening carefully, Ellie realized that Wayne was praying a prayer too deep for human language. She had heard her mother pray like this. A travailing prayer, she called it. The beautiful sound like soothing music so comforted her aching heart that she fell into a restful sleep that called up no torturing dreams.

When she roused again, darkness had forsaken the room. She hurried to wash and dress, coiling her hair into a tight knot on the back of her head. Tiny golden ringlets refused to be restrained, though, and curled about her pinched face and the nape of her neck. The girl who looked back at her from the brass looking glass wore little hollows in her cheeks, the price of her weighted heart. The threat of tears still badgered her red-rimmed eyelids. Facing a day had never posed so great a challenge. Her only reason for gladness was that Beatrice Webster could not possibly come home in the swirling snowstorm.

Footsteps in the adjoining room indicated that she had overslept. Her brothers, the unthoughtful, careless fellows of the past, had been quiet so as not to awaken her. They could not know that her heart had . . . died.

She goaded herself on toward the kitchen; it would take awhile for her to start the fire in the iron cookstove to prepare breakfast. Would her arms lift the iron lids? A body must be driven on in spite of the missing heart. She wasn't the first one to suffer such desolation, she reminded herself, nor would be the last.

She looked about, confused. The teakettle whistled, sending a cloud of pearly steam toward the ceiling, offering hot water for tea. The milk buckets were missing. Wayne had readied the stove for cooking, put on the water to boil, and gone to the cow lot to milk the cows for her. The man who brought her greatest sorrow by his story of Daniel found so many ways to lift her burden. The irony of it all brought a pitiful twitch to Ellie's lips.

Empty. That's what life would be without the dream of Daniel's eventual return. The future would be . . . There would be no future for her. Only a past. Only a carved heart on a tree. A wooden heart.

She looked out the window and watched Wayne stamp his snow-covered boots on the back stoop. A snowball flew from somewhere and smashed him on the neck. He set the bucket down carefully to one side and started forming great balls of packed snow for repayment, grinning a crooked smile. Suddenly, the air was filled with whizzing white balls and shrieks of laughter. Wayne was good for her brothers.

Willy came in first, peeling off his coat. "Wayne said

he would make us some snow ice cream today, Ellie. Won't that be nice?"

"Ummmm . . . hummmmm." Her voice trailed off. Engulfed by the final loss of all that mattered to her, she suddenly felt as frozen as the icicles hanging from the eaves in long spears of solid ice.

Her dream died last evening.

CHAPTER NINE
The Journal

---

*I*n hardback, the journal cost forty-nine cents, an extravagant price to pay for a diary, and Ellie wondered where her mother got the money to buy it. Perhaps it had been a gift.

Why Ellie sought out this long-forgotten ledger now she could not consciously justify. But a hunger stirred by Wayne's prayer caused her to wonder if her mother had recorded Ellie's baptism there.

She had been asleep but had awakened abruptly. Taking her lamp into the parlor, she dug into the old trunk. The bound memories would be in the bottom right-hand corner.

Mary Webster kept an individual section on each of her five children, doing her best to capture memorable events with her pen and imprison them on the pages of the journal.

Ellie hastily scanned through the boys' biographies first. A firstborn son's heritage, Travis's chapter dripped with details that could only ignite the interest of a doting mother: the first tooth . . . the first word . . . the first step. Too poor to own a camera, Mary painted word pictures. "Travis saw the cow chewing her cud and thought she was making preparations to eat him," one page said. His chapter was almost filled. The last few pages left blank, were probably reserved for his first date, his marriage, his children.

Jimmy's chapter was less exact. Instead of precise dates, notations were written in relative figures. "Jimmy began to walk at about eleven months. He was running all over the house at one year."

With Willy, Mrs. Webster must have been busier and less inclined to notice baby antics handed down from two previous infants. His portion of the book wasn't half filled.

Even less was said about Walter, the last son. Hurried, incomplete sentences ran across the pages. But even at that, the motherly love was still in evidence. Mary loved all her children.

With Ellie it was different. It seemed Mary had lived a lifetime to mother a daughter, and her pen spilled that proclamation onto the paper in paragraphs of delight. Ellie's chapter was entitled "Lest I Forget."

"Dear daughter," it began, "before you were born, when friends would ask, 'Do you want a boy or a girl?' I couldn't answer, 'It doesn't matter,' like other mothers. Because it did matter. It mattered very much. I wanted a daughter. All my life I wanted a daughter. For to have a daughter is to live all over again. To laugh again. To cry again. To hurt again. To win again.

"The day of your birth is one of the most pleasurable moments in the magic called memory. Thinking of it as I write this, I still feel the bubble of excitement, the tingle of joy, the warmth of fulfillment.

"Surely it was a selfish wish—this wish for one of my own kind. I wanted life to give me a daughter. So God gave me you.

"The years will come and go—oh, so swiftly—in a succession of physical and spiritual unfolding, each year growing sweeter than the one before.

"Some day, my little Ellie, you will make a home of your own. I wish nothing greater for you than the happiness of true love—and a daughter. So that you may live all over again. And laugh again. And cry again. And hurt again. And win again.

"For to have a daughter . . . is never to die."

A tear fell onto the brittle page. *The laughter is past,* Ellie thought, *and most of the crying. I've made it to the hurting. But oh, Mother, did you ever win? And will I ever win?*

Yes, her mother had won. She had won a crown of everlasting life.

Ellie skipped past records of her first tooth gained and her first tooth lost, past starting school with her hair plaited into French braids tied with ribbons that matched her pinafore, and past her first report card with a D in conduct.

Had her mother recorded the revival where Ellie received the experience that changed her heart? How old had she been? Ten? Eleven? Twelve? She couldn't remember. Some said that childrens' stories should not be taken at face value. But what happened to her was no figment of her imagination.

She scanned the pages. Her mother's writing was smaller here, crowding more details into her history than into that of the others. Yes, there it was!

"Ellie and I went to revival tonight. My daughter has a thirst for knowledge about God with questions that I cannot answer. I thought the traveling preacher might help her.

"It was Ellie who received the biblical revelation of who Jesus really is. 'The God who saved Daniel from the lions and the Hebrew children from the fire came to earth as a man named Jesus,' she told me.

"I said, no, that God and Jesus were two different people. And the Holy Ghost was a third person. They all three live in heaven, and when I pray to each of them, I try not to play favorites but give each equal time.

"Ellie looked at me with a sort of sadness. 'But, Mother, God is a *Spirit*. He's everywhere. He's right here with me and you. Don't you see? That Spirit was in Jesus, making Him God on earth. That's why He could do all those wonderful miracles! And the Holy Spirit isn't another person, but the Spirit of the one God. He came into my heart tonight. There's just one God, and his name is Jesus. That's why the preacher said it is so important to be baptized in His name. Jesus came in His Father's name, you see. So the *name* of the Father, Son, and Holy Ghost is Jesus. Please, Mother, may I be baptized in Jesus' name?' "

Ellie remembered the conversation, the thrill of truth as it burst on her soul. Her mother agreed to her baptism, and the preacher took Ellie to the creek, along with her mother and a dozen more, to wash her sins away. She could still feel the clean sensation.

As long as Mary Webster lived, they went to the annual brush-arbor meetings together. But after her mother went to claim her crown, the cares of life drowned Ellie. Chill bumps prickled across Ellie's arms now. Winter's cold breath crept into the room. The stove had lost its cherry glow as the fire settled to embers.

What is happening in this room happened in my heart. Ellie closed the journal and faced her cold-numbed soul. *Once I had the glow of the Spirit inside keeping me warm. I've let the fire die out. I need to stoke it up . . . add some fuel. . . .*

CHAPTER TEN

The Listener

The week of the blizzard would have been pleasant enough had Ellie not been dead at heart. The boys played at snow wars, pulled taffy, and made snow ice cream—and tried to include her. For their sakes, she wanted to cooperate, but her spirit flagged.

One night Wayne asked for a Bible, and when she produced her mother's, he handled it with such meticulous care and reverence that it moved her. He read Ezekiel's account of the potter's wheel and closed the Book.

"I once saw a potter working at a wheel," he said. The boys pulled their chairs closer to listen. "It fascinated me. First, the potter kneaded the clay in his hands gently until there were no lumps at all. Then he splattered it on the wheel with a great force. After that, he started the big wheel spinning faster and faster. With pressure from his thumb and his fingers, he shaped and molded the clay." Wayne demonstrated with his work-worn hands. "I was amazed at the beautiful piece of pottery he created from that piece of earth."

The boys asked questions, and Wayne answered them, sagaciously leading the story to its spiritual climax without losing the boys' attention. "Sometimes, when our head is in a spin, we feel that the Great Potter has lost the pattern to our lives," he said, "but He hasn't." He handed the Bible back to Ellie as if reluctant to relinquish it.

"You make the Bible seem real, Wayne," Walter complimented. "Ellie can do that, too." He shifted his gaze. "I've been meaning to ask you, Ellie: what happened to that pretty wall picture you made with the Ten Commandments on it?" He pinned her to the wall with eyes that demanded an answer.

"I-I moved it?"

"Why?"

Dare she tell him? She had never been untruthful with any of the boys. "It . . . offended Beatrice, Walter."

"Hoity-toity! The Ten Commandments offend *her?* I rather think *she* offends the Ten Commandments!"

On the seventh day, the sun came out, the weather warmed considerably, and the snow began its melting process. Mr. Webster would be bringing Beatrice home any time now. Ellie sensed the atmosphere growing rigid, like a violin string pulled tighter and tighter, ready to snap. Meals became sessions of smoldering resentment. No one wished to mention the homecoming, as if by ignoring the dread event it might not materialize.

Wayne moved his scant belongings back to the barn. Something holy moved out with him, leaving Ellie's chafed emotions to suffer a dull, unplaced desolation. He had brought a degree of comfort, security. Especially were his night prayers a solace. He had met her Daniel; he knew her God. She did not recognize the moral support he brought to her until he closed the door behind him and she heard the crunch of his boots fade out of earshot.

The coming of a new and godless authority in the home, the anxiety she felt for her brothers' futures, and the news of Daniel's death all came crashing in on Ellie. Waves of hot anger and cold fear converged to harrow her reeling mind. A thousand thronging sensations came and went. Betrayal. Despair. Incredulity. Dread. Confusion. Her mind darted from one dead-end road to another. She felt like a cornered thing with no place of refuge. Her room would be taken, her personal liberties desecrated. There would be no privacy to pray, to meditate . . . to remember.

A thousand ages of time separated her from Daniel. Even his face blurred in the layers of weary months that stacked between her and the last sight of him. The letter! That would bring back his cheerful side, lasso her senses back into focus, ease the pain. To see his handwriting, to hold the pages he penned: That was the answer. *Just one more moment with my dream before I lay it away forever, God!*

She found the letter, held it to her breast, and kissed it with trembling lips. It was her funeral service for Daniel, his last rites. Only a marker, carved on the pulpy trunk of a tree, remained to her.

What recourse had she now? She might have moved to the Brock home place and lived out her life there alone, there where Daniel once ate and slept and prayed, had not the Greaves took residence in the cabin. But now, with the Brocks dead, the Greaves would be free to stay on endlessly. Nobody would contest their right to be there. If she could only have foreseen this day three months ago and told Mr. Greaves that she would be occupying the house herself!

The dam of her reserve broke, and tears splashed onto her faded calico pinafore and onto the letter. God had surely lost the pattern for her life! Holding to the most tangible thing she had left of Daniel, she allowed the great sobs that pulled at her throat to wrack her body—soul-deep sobs, as one would weep at the wake of a departed companion.

She neither saw nor heard Wayne enter the back door. He stood beside her, lightly touching her shoulder. Her hand flew to the letter in her lap to cover it. "Is something wrong, miss?"

She looked up, and seeing that it was Wayne, tried to smear the tears away with the back of her hand. "I'm . . . sorry. I didn't know anyone—"

"Please don't apologize." He seemed embarrassed that he had caught her crying. "I owe the apologies to you for coming in unannounced. I . . . left something in the attic room."

"But . . . I shouldn't be such a foolish crybaby."

"As I see it, you've had more than your share of hardships, Miss Webster. I hope that I'm not adding to your burden. I wish I might be more help. If there's any little way I can lift your load . . ."

"Oh, you have already! My . . . tears . . . have nothing to do with *you*. Really. It's just that I . . . I . . . the one that I loved is . . . *d-dead* and . . ." Her voice snagged on thorns of grief. "I was just r-reading the letter he wrote me. Just a few weeks ago I found it in the vacated house . . . ."

"I understand, miss." Ellie thought his voice would

break. "I lost my only true love, too. We were very happy with each other and with our God. She and I were parted by a terrible tragedy. And I find that I can never love another like I loved her."

"See," Ellie reproached herself with a teary half-smile, "here I cry for me when others are hurting, too. I'm ashamed that you caught me indulging in self-pity, sir. I'm sorry for your loss." *He's lost a wife. And maybe a child, too,* she told herself. *His grief is deeper than my own. His heart has died, too. I know that I'll never have to worry about any romantic notions on his part. We can just be comrades in misery. And how I need a friend now!*

"Was it Daniel Brock that you loved? One of your brothers mentioned—"

"Oh, yes, sir, it was. How I loved him! We planned to be married when he returned. He . . . he carved a heart on a tree for me. Then his family moved away before we had a chance to say goodbye. I've been waiting all these years for him to return for me. And when I heard you tell Travis about the . . . the massacre, . . . I just wanted to die, too." She bit her lower lip to stop its quivering.

"Believe me, miss. I know what it's like to bury a dream. And even if I could . . . forget the past, who would want a deformed thing like this?" He pointed to his twisted face. "I'm not sorry for the scars. I could not have lived with myself if I had done . . . .less. But could I give a child this sort of a father to look upon?"

"But your soul isn't scarred, sir, like . . . like Jed Greaves's. I know that you must be a Christian, and that's what matters."

"Yes, my love and I dedicated our lives to the Lord when we were both young. She had a God-fearing mother, and so did I. An elderly Spirit-filled parson came through our country and led us to the wonderful gift of salvation."

"Daniel was a Christian, too. He was the most *honest* man I've ever met. Why, he'd rather die than lie. He talked to me many times about what was good and right and true. He once said to me, 'Ellie, dishonesty always costs more than it's worth, but honesty is always worth more than it costs.' The more I thought on that, the bigger it got. Daniel said that the truth is what made men free, and anyone who wasn't honest with God, himself, and his fellow man was a slave to shameful disgrace."

"Yes, that sounds like something Daniel Brock might have said. That's just the way he thought."

"He said there were only two roads—the high road and the low road—and that there was no in-between. Either a person was clean and honest, or he was a coward. The world lost a real man when it lost Daniel."

"A real man is never lost, ma'am. The influence he has on others never dies."

"I'd . . . I'd never thought of it that way. Daniel helped me to find my way to God, so if what you say is true, as long as I am alive, Daniel will really never die."

"That's right."

"Without what Daniel taught me about God, I—I don't think I could have made it this far. But this—this woman that my father has married wants nothing to do with God or religion." Unshed tears glistened in Ellie's violet eyes. "She's—she's worldly. She even wants to take away the memories of our sweet little Christian mother. And right now when the boys need spiritual guidance so badly, . . ."

"Remember what I said the other night, miss? God

hasn't lost the pattern to your lives. He's the Master Potter. It won't be easy, but we have Someone to lean upon."

The snort of horses warned Ellie of the dreaded arrival of her father and his wife. She threw back the sash in time to see the buggy, wearing a thick skin of mud, bump over the cattle guard, throwing Beatrice against Mr. Webster.

Wayne scuttled up the ladder and down again with a roll of clothing. "I'll pray for you, Miss Webster," he said. Then he was gone before Mr. Webster and Beatrice reached the porch.

"I hope Ellie has some of that good berry pie made for me, Ronald," the heavy woman said. "I'm famished!"

"I'm sure Ellie didn't know what day we would be coming back, sweetie. And, oh yes, I heard her say that she used the last jar of berries on our wedding meal."

"No more berries? No more berry pies? The very idea! Why didn't she put up plenty, Ronald? With the woods full of berries, it was very careless of her not to can enough to last for a year."

"Well, with feeding so many . . ."

"And just imagine, Ronald. What if I had been stuck here in this isolated place for seven whole days with no berry pie, not a single novel to read, and without my solitaire!"

The voice of Beatrice defiled the snow-washed air. "Why, I might have died of boredom!"

CHAPTER ELEVEN
Mrs. Trouble

---

*E*llie dipped her fingers into a bowl of water and flicked sprinkles onto the stiffly starched clothes, rolling them into a ball to dampen for ironing. Beatrice dressed in a fresh frock every day, doubling Ellie's usual dozen in the clothes basket.

"*Eleanor!*"

"Yes, ma'am?"

"Fix me a cup of hot tea."

Ellie's dripping fingers stopped their shaking in midair, little balls of water forming on their tips. She dried her hands, set the sadiron on the stove to heat, and then poured her stepmother's tea.

"And, Eleanor—"

"Yes?"

"Make it with one lump of sugar and plenty of cream."

Beatrice's puffy eyes tattled that she had just awakened. It was near noon. She padded into the kitchen, her coarse black hair askew, her large nose shiny.

"The holidays are past now, Eleanor." She sipped her tea, forgetting to thank Ellie. "It's time we make a constructive work schedule for the year ahead. Your father tells me that you have quite a few outside chores. He says it is your job to go to the well for water, milk the cows, and gather the eggs from the henhouse."

She yawned and waited for Ellie's confirmation.

Ellie hesitated, cowing under Beatrice's blinkless stare. "I, well, actually, the hired man has been doing most of my outdoor work for me during the cold weather."

"I see. He has his own work to do, though: repairing fences, feeding the livestock, and turning the fields for planting. With spring coming on now, he'll be quite busy. So we'll leave those chores I mentioned chargeable to you. And I'll do the inside work. *Except* breakfast and the ironing, of course. I have to have my morning rest, and ironing hurts my back.

"We'll start our new plan today. I will prepare the evening meal while you iron. I'll be needing my blue cheviot. Your father and I need to go into town for supplies soon. I'll see what you have in the pantry and what's lacking. I like plenty of refined sugar, spices, and flavoring when I cook. I don't care for your wheat flour; I prefer bleached flour. The mercantile will have the supplies that I need."

Ellie wondered where her father would find the money for the luxuries this woman demanded. She had scrimped and saved all winter to make ends meet, and the items Beatrice suggested were expensive. Walter and Jimmy both needed school shoes, and Travis's one shirt gave witness to many Mondays spent in the wash pot, obviously not immune to shrinking. Layers of patches made an amusing checkerboard of newer blues and washed-out neutrals. She had mentioned their needs to her father recently.

Beatrice had her first meal on the table when the men gathered at dusk. She pottered about, shuffling from the cookstove to the side cupboard and back again, accomplishing little. Her round, red face disclosed that she wasn't accustomed to such exertion over a hot stove. She sat down with a self-satisfied smile. Mr. Webster patted her rotund arm and forgot to say grace.

Walter started the disastrous conversation. "Ellie, I never knew you to make such *lumpy* gravy! It's not fit to eat! And no *salt!*" He looked to her for an explanation.

With her finger to her mouth, she threw him a silent warning, but he missed it. "Walter, I didn't—"

"If you think th' gravy's bad, Walt, wait til you taste th' *beans*. They're scorched to a burnt sacrifice! They taste too bad to eat." Willy made a wry face. "Where was your *mind,* Ellie?"

"An' this biscuit is as hard as a *rock,*" chimed in Jimmy. "Look!" He held up the overbaked knot of unleavened dough and dropped it on the table with an awful thud.

"What are you tryin' to do, Ellie?" Travis teased, poking at his sister with his elbow. "Kill us all with this *slop?*"

Something pulled Ellie's attention toward Wayne. Merriment was written on his distorted features. His one good eye danced, telling her he knew what had happened. "But just taste those pickled cucumbers, boys. Yum! They make the meal."

"Th' dessert had better be good," Walter complained, "or we'll fire the cook!"

Beatrice had had enough. She jumped up from the

table, her arms akimbo and her small, black eyes flashing fire. "There *is* no dessert!" she yelled. "*I* cooked the meal, and you'll eat it or do without! And I will be cooking your supper from *now on.*"

No one dared say a word. No one moved. Ellie thought Willie looked greenish gray around the mouth. Jimmy pushed back his plate with the gravy, more like dumplings, only half eaten. He looked as though he might lose what he had already consumed any minute.

Beatrice had eaten little of the unappetizing meal herself. She left in a huff, and Mr. Webster followed her to her room to make amends.

"Listen, Ellie," Jimmy whispered savagely when they were gone, "if we have to eat this garbage, we'll *starve.* I'd rather eat *grass* like Nebuchadnezzar. Do ya think you could fix extra biscuits for breakfast so's we can slip a few of them to our room?"

"She makes the rules in this house now. You'll have to learn to like her cooking, Jimmy."

He groaned. "Not in a million years, Ellie!"

The next morning, Ellie made an extra pan of biscuits, and they disappeared into overall bibs and coat pockets while Mr. Webster wasn't looking. Wayne grinned and slipped one into each of his work gloves.

Ellie's head pounded from the strain that hung in the air like deadly fumes. Her heart throbbed like a muffled bongo drum. She tiptoed to the room she now shared with Walter and Willy and buried her burning face in a pillow. *God, where is the pattern for our lives?* she wept.

A door slammed, and feet shuffled in the adjoining bedroom, Beatrice's room. Ellie heard the scrape of a

chair, then voices, hushed but clearly audible.
"Did you enjoy your breakfast, Ronald?" A peel of sugary sarcasm coated the sour words beneath it.
"Yes, sweetie, I did. Ellie is a good cook. She does have the boys rather spoilt. But they will get used to your cooking. One can't expect you to cook your style without the ingredients you need, of course. They didn't know you cooked the meal, or they would never have said a word to offend you. Ellie will be glad to cook our evening meals until—"
"No! They can like it or lump it! When I make a rule, I don't back down. It's Ellie this and Ellie that until I'm sick of it! I'll be glad when Eleanor is *gone.*"
"But she isn't going anywhere, dear," Was Mr. Webster's patience with this petulant woman assumed or real? "She hasn't anywhere to go."
"Well, we'll *find* her somewhere to go. No house is large enough for two women—"
"Why, Beatrice, Ellie is my daughter, and this is her home for as long as she wishes to live here. I explained that to you from the start, before we were married."
"Ronald, you've mollycoddled and overprotected your children shamefully! You have done them no favor by tying them to your suspenders. You should—you *must*— start pushing them from the nest. Make them independent. We no longer live in the dark ages. Modern young people know their way about in the world by the time they reach the age of accountability. I should think Eleanor would be considering marriage by now, instead of being a liability to her father and a blight to his newfound happiness. Imagine! A young lady going on twenty-two and still single and stodgy!"

"Beatrice! Ellie never has to marry unless she wishes to."

"She *wishes* to. All girls do. We'll *find* someone for her to marry. She's smart and pretty. We should have little trouble."

"How?"

"We'll invite young men in to visit. She'll never become betrothed if prospective suitors don't even know she's alive."

There was a long silence, a silence that demanded to be toppled.

"And I'll tell you one thing, Ronald: if we don't do something soon, I foresee serious trouble."

"Between yourself and Ellie?"

"No. Between Eleanor and your hired man. Do you realize that he has been doing her chores for her all winter just to win her favor?"

"Wayne? I'm sure you are mistaken, Bea."

"I'm not mistaken. Ask her. She told me with her own mouth that he had. She might just up and marry him. Have you thought of that?"

"I don't think there's a possibility, sweetie. You see, Ellie had a sweetheart in her younger years and he—broke her heart."

"Broken hearts make the worst of rebounds."

"Well, Wayne is a man of integrity. If Ellie should fall in love with him, and he with her, it might not be such a bad match. I hadn't thought of it until now. I rather like the idea."

"*Ronald Webster!* You mean you would allow a daughter of yours to marry an ugly-faced thing like *that?*"

Ellie winced at the cruelty of Beatrice's words.

"Man looks on the outward appearance, Beatrice, but God looks on the heart. Wayne has a heart of pure gold."

"Don't talk to me about God, Ronald. If there's a God at all, He's in heaven, and I'm down here. He takes care of the stars and the moon and the sun, and He expects us to see after ourselves below. That's why He gave us brains. I'd be mortified to introduce that man, a homeless waif, a drifter, as my son-in-law. Has he money? Has he a social standing?" She didn't wait for an answer. "I thought not. He's a nothing. A *nobody*."

Beatrice had worked herself up into a pitch that wasn't hushed now.

"Shhh, sweetie. Ellie was out of the kitchen when I came in, but she might come back into the house and hear us."

"It might be good if she did," scorned Beatrice. "I see that you are a softie, Ronald. I want you to let Wayne go as soon as the crops are planted."

"But, dear, I could never find a man that will work so hard for so little wages. And with the boys in school . . ."

"I want Eleanor to marry into a higher echelon of society than a barn dweller. Her patrician beauty begs ball dresses and ermine shawls. And I don't want anybody around to botch my plans. These favors your hired hand does for Eleanor are not done for the man's health! He must go."

"But you don't understand, Beatrice. Ellie is a farm girl. She isn't the society type. She wouldn't fit in society."

"How can you know that? Every girl has a built-in want for the finer things of life. It's buried so deeply in some that they don't even know it is there. You—and her mother—made her the way she is by sheltering her, hiding her way out here in the sticks, and giving her no chance at self-expression."

Ellie clenched her fists. How dare this blackhearted woman to criticize her righteous mother's child-rearing methods?

"Leave it to me, dear." Beatrice's voice might have been that of Satan himself. "I know about bringing up a daughter in our changing world. I will start to work on Eleanor. Subtly, of course. She has a most sensitive nature, but I'll soon have her thinking that my ideas, my decisions, are her own." She gave a coarse-grained laugh. "And since I've been awakened at this ungodly hour, we may as well make the trip into town today for supplies."

"But I was planning—"

"I must have my supplies before I cook another meal, Ronald. I will not be humiliated again!"

Ellie crept back to the kitchen, soul-weary and sick of heart. What trap of the devil lay ahead for her now? And how could she escape it?

"Eleanor . . ." Ellie could not bring herself to look into Beatrice's powdered face. "Your father and I are going to town for groceries. We may be gone for a couple of days. I will want to see Wancille and Julius. And I must go to the bookstore for some new novels. I'll bring you back a big catalogue from the mail-order house so that you can have a look at some of the bustles that are in style this year. We need to update your wardrobe. Don't worry, though, I'll tear out the pages of underwear and keep them in my room. You'd think them obscene. But I rather enjoy peeking at them myself."

Ellie felt a deep crimson stain her cheeks. She

clamped her teeth together to imprison her tongue. She dare not trust herself to let a single word slip through the ivory prison at this moment.

Beatrice swept out the door to join Mr. Webster, and Ellie heard the carriage rattle over the rough cattle guard.

Willy burst through the back door, his fingers shaped in a victory sign. "Let's pray for another snowstorm, Ellie! And could you start cooking us some supper now? We're pinin' away for some of *your* bread and gravy. And may we have a custard with meringue for dessert, please?"

He started out the door. On an impish impulse, he called back, "You know what me and Walter call her? *Mrs. Trouble!*"

CHAPTER TWELVE
A New Worry

---

*E*llie leaned her head against the high back of the rocker, the sting of her stepmother's words still digging deep trenches in her soul.

"The mother eagle pushes the eaglet from the nest. Then, before it crashes to the ground, she swoops under it and lifts it up." The words from one of Ellie's beloved childhood stories told to her by her own mother brought comfort to her as a small girl. But now it seemed that she had fallen and splattered so many times that all her bones were in the wrong places. And who was to care when she fell, utterly destroyed? Where were God's "wings"?

Beatrice said that she should marry. There was merit to the woman's reasoning. What did the years ahead hold for a girl who never wed, never had any children . . . or grandchildren? Daniel was dead. The heart on the tree would gradually fade with time. Might she request to be buried in a solitary grave beneath the tree?

A rap on the door brought her head up with an abrupt

snap. Who would be calling at this time of the day? Wayne was in the far field plowing. Had one of the boys been injured at school? Hastily, and with unsteady hands, Ellie unlatched the front door.

A shoddy woman with bold eyes stood waiting for an invitation to enter. Ellie hesitated.

"May I please come in, miss?"

Ellie stepped aside. What sort of woman would be traveling alone? And at this time of year?

"Hello. I'm Mazie Greaves. Wife of old man Greaves that lives next over." She gave her thumb an unladylike jerk in the direction of the Brock property. "Guess we'll be livin' there from now on till judgment day. It sorta suits my old man's fancy. So I thought I'd best come an' interdooce myself. Jed said a mere girl run this here place single-handed. Lawsy, girl, how do you manage it?"

"You are Jed's mother?"

"Lawsy, girl, do I look *that* old? Jed's most nigh as old as I am."

Ellie blushed, stumbling on an apology. With Mazie's youngish face and flabby body, she might be anywhere between twenty and fifty. "I thought . . . well, I—"

"I don't mean to confuse you. Jed is my husband's son, see. Not mine."

Ellie recalled Mr. Greaves's reference to a previous marriage.

"Greaves had a whole passel o' kids by his first woman. She up and left him. I can't say as I blame her with all them younguns to care for. Part o' the bunch lives with Greaves's maw back in Tennessee. I shore wasn't fixin' to take an' raise that many! No siree. We moved here to get away from 'um. I shore hope they don't up and try to foller us. Only Jed came along with us. He was th' oldest. We figgered he could help out money wise. Beats anything you ever saw for makin' money. He never goes into town but what he comes away without money in his pocket from somewhere. Yep, it beats it all!"

Ellie nodded, not knowing how to respond to her unwanted guest.

"My mama, now, she didn't want me to marry Greaves. He's *ages* older than me. But my beau was a trifling sort, and I decided to show him a thing or two. Was he ever surprised when he learned that I'd up and married old man Greaves! Just one week from 'Howdy do' to 'I do.' The poor fish I was courtin' ain't never quit pinin' for me till this very day. But it's good enough for him." Mazie broke off. "Lawsy, you got *six* menfolks to feed?"

"Yes, and until yesterday I did the cooking for all of them. But my father married back before Christmas, and my stepmother has just begun to help with the meals. She prepared the supper last evening."

"There's five brothers besides your papa?"

"I only have four brothers. The other is a hired hand."

"That's the big boy with the bad eye?"

"Yes, ma'am."

"Jed don't like him much. I don't know why, though. He seems awful handy to me. Why, he even cut and stacked some wood for us. Jed's not keen on cuttin' wood. And you know what else your hired man said he would do? He said he'd plant a garden for me. A big, nice one. Jed don't like plantin' neither." She gave a raucous laugh. "I make it sound as if Jed don't like doin' *no* work, don't I? Well, he likes townish stuff. He's plannin' on bein' a store tender or runnin' a night joint. He says that's where th' money rolls. He's kinda took a shine to you, I think. He said he plans on takin' you to town an' showin' you what real life is all about. He's good at showin' girls around. I think he kinda sorrows for you bein' all stuck out here with no chance to get a peek at th' city world. 'Wastin' a lot of pretty girl' is the way he put it."

"Oh, I'm sure I'll live and die right here, Mrs. Greaves. I have no hankering for city life."

Mazie gave a careless wave of her hand. "Jed needs a good woman to do his work for him. I'm gonna get tired of waiting on him hand and hoof by-me-by. One man's enough to slave for."

Ellie said nothing.

"Where's your mama?"

"She's gone to her mansion."

"Her *mansion?* You mean to tell me you are rich folks? Jed will be glad to hear—"

"I mean, Mrs. Greaves, that my mother has died and gone to heaven. And yes, we're rich. At least, I am. I have a great inheritance waiting for me."

"You don't say?"

"But not in this world."

"Jed ain't interested in pie in the sky."

"What a pity."

"It was your stepmama I was inquiring about really. Where is she?"

"She and my father went into town for supplies."

"Well, I came to ask her—"

"You'll have to come back in a couple of days, Mrs. Greaves. I expect they'll be gone today and tomorrow."

"What I came to ask concerns you, miss . . . what's your name?"

"Ellie."

". . . Ellie. You could call me Mazie if you want to. *Mrs. Greaves* sounds like a name for an old lady. And I dare say I ain't a whit older than yourself. I really came to ask a neighborly favor of you."

"Yes?"

"The husband and I need to go into town ourselves to draw up some papers on the place over there. We'd only be gone half a day. I was wondering if you could possibly tend the baby while I am gone."

"The baby?"

"Yes. Greaves and I have a baby. She's six months old. I don't want to take her out. She's too much trouble on town trips. And Jed isn't handy at keeping bawlin' babies. In fact, I need to hurry right on home now, or Jed will walk right out an' leave her in her crib. Please be at my house by eight o'clock in the mornin'. That'll give you plenty of time to feed your six men—or I guess it's just five with your papa gone—and get your brothers off to school. Are they all in school?"

"Yes, ma'am."

"Lawsy, seems some of them are too big to still be in school! Why, Jed cut out of school when he first turned a teenager, his paw said. Anyway, we should be back by the time school lets out. Don't be late, or Greaves will be out of patience with me. And how he cusses and raves when he runs out of patience!"

"But . . . I've never . . . taken care of a baby. That is, not since Walter. I was only ten when he was born."

"Nothin' to it. With girls it just comes natural. I'll show you how to pin on didies an' fix sugar in a rag for a passie when you get there tomorrow. If *I* learned, you can learn. I gotta go now." She left on the run, calling back, "I'll repay th' favor someday, Ellie."

Ellie yielded herself to the tempting lure of the rocking chair in which to think. It wasn't that she minded tending the baby or doing a neighborly turn. But would she be aiding and abetting the Greaves' scheme to seize the Brock property? And could she bear the long hours of being alone with the child in Daniel's home place? The last time she was there, she had found the letter. She dropped her head into her hands. *How . . . can . . . I . . . bear . . . it, . . . Daniel?*

When the storm of emotion had blustered by, she pulled herself from the chair and went to the kitchen to churn the cream, hoping that the rhythmic splat and slurp of the wooden dasher in the tall ironstone churn would provide the needed therapy for her jangled nerves. The golden cream, skimmed from many containers of cool milk, was thicker than syrup. Mr. Webster mentioned purchasing a separator and a newfangled churn with a paddle and a crank handle. But Ellie knew that she would miss the old method of producing butter. Beatrice said she was old-fashioned; Beatrice was right.

As she gripped the smooth handle in both of her hands, pulling it up and plunging it down, a concerned voice near the back door arrested her attention.

"Jimmy, why didn't you go to school today?"

"Me an' Jed's goin' in to town."

"It might be best to wait and ask permission of your father. Does he know that you are going?"

"Paw'll never even know I went. He's too wrapped up in his pie-faced 'sweetie' to care a shard for me! Jed said he could get me a little job that would make big bucks

in a hurry. I'll be back afore Paw gets home."
"What sort of work is it, Jimmy? Is it *honest* work?"
"I don't know what kind of work it is. Actually, I'll just be helpin' Jed, and he'll split the payroll with me. That's th' deal. How could you beat that?"
"I don't like the sounds of it, Jimmy. Jed hasn't the scruples I'd like to see a young man have." Wayne's voice faded with distance.
"I promised him I'd go and help him out, and I'm a man of my word. So I'm going."
The paddle stopped in the ocean of cream. Here was a brand-new worry for Ellie's tired mind.

CHAPTER THIRTEEN

The Wings

"Bring yourself right on in," Mazie called, not bothering to open the door for Ellie. "I knowed you'd be on time. I told Greaves you was that dependable sort. I could just tell by lookin'!"

"I promised the boys at breakfast that I would be back in time to serve their supper."

"Oh, sure. We'll be home aplenty ahead of that."

A nauseous wave of sickness swept through Ellie's whole being. She wanted to retrace her steps, to get away. Would she ever overcome this black, empty feeling when she entered Daniel's home?

She saw that the Greaves made free use of what remained of the Brock furniture, giving another's possessions little consideration. The table was clothless, cluttered with dirty dishes. Water rings that had not been dried defaced the wooden surface. The throw rug, under which she had found Daniel's letter, held layers of mud.

"I said I'd show you about the baby's care, Ellie. I fold Dee's didies in a triangle like this." Mazie Greaves folded a gauzy diaper into a three-cornered shape. "And then I pin it in the front with one big pin. Some of th' modern gals fold in a square, but that takes two pins, one on each side. Lawsy, what a waste! When Dee is wet, just take off the soppy diadie and hang it on the back of a cane-bottom chair to dry. I use 'um over and over. I only wash the dirty ones."

"Where is the baby?"

"She's still asleep."

"Where will I find her food?"

"I fed her good afore she went to sleep. She'll get hungry afore I get back. Lawsy, seems she stays hungry most of the time! But just give her the sugar rag to suck on. She'll survive. Most do."

Mazie slung off her dingy apron, threw it across a chair, and made a dash for the door, grabbing her handbag in one grand swoop. It seemed to Ellie that this girl-woman of indeterminate age moved in a fast waddle everywhere she went.

Mazie was a poor housekeeper. Dust choked the curtains, and crumbs powdered the floor beneath the table, inviting mice. Ellie could not sit, nor her hands lie idle, with such rampant filth. Cleanliness clung to her nature, and she began cleaning the place at once. Mrs. Brock would turn over in her grave if she could see her home so neglected! Mrs. Brock . . . dead, murdered by outlaws. As a memorial to the immaculate housewife of the past, Ellie put things in order as the deceased woman would have wished them.

Feverish scrubbing had used up about an hour of time before the baby stirred and began to whimper. Ellie put aside the mop, washed her hands carefully with lye soap, and went into the baby's room—the room that had once been Daniel's.

The wonder of the child swallowed all dread when Ellie saw the sleepy face, topped with a tousle of curls. Such a miniature of beauty! How could something so . . . so lovely come from such a slatternly mother?

The baby gave Ellie a winsome and trusting smile, making a gurgle of delight. Anyone would relish caring for this doll-like infant! She gathered the child into her unaccustomed arms, letting a tear fall onto the downy head. A soft hand reached up to pat Ellie's neck. No wonder Jesus said, "For of such is the kingdom of heaven."

Above the silky hair, Ellie's vision focused on a heart carved on a panel of the wall. The heart, larger than the one on the tree by the well but identical in design, had once borne her initials and Daniel's. Now a fresh cut pierced through Daniel's initials, and a crude "J. G." was whittled in. The work of Jed Greaves.

Ellie held the baby close to stop the fierce outcry of her wounded spirit. She hurried from the room, fleeing anger and hatred, struggling desperately to keep her soul free from a wretched hostility that threatened to obsess her. How dare Jed do such a spiteful thing!

Please, God, . . . come with the wings. . . . I'm about to crash. . . . The words seemed to her a dying plea rather than a prayer. Once she fought from the outside in, now she fought from the inside out.

To still the inner raging, she rocked the baby back and forth and sang. At first, her motions were frenzied, hurried, unpatterned. But gradually, the impromptu songs and her swaying became soft and sweet. She had never imagined that holding a child, a precious gift of God, could bring such peace to a troubled mind. If only she could hold this baby near her breast forever! While she crooned and the baby made smacking noises on her own small fist, the fast beat of approaching steps reached her ears. She supposed that the Greaves had decided against their trip to town after all and were returning. Or perhaps they had forgotten something.

The door swung open abruptly. Jed stood facing her, a wicked grin wreathing his proud face. "Oh, I thought so, kitten," he said. "I thought I'd find you here. Now it's me that can purr. I've got you all to myself at last. How could I be so lucky?"

A sinister foreboding silenced the lullaby Ellie hummed. All trace of music vanished, leaving a chilling suspense. At the sight of Jed, the child clung to Ellie in apparent terror, beginning to cry.

"Your help is not needed here." Ellie fought hard to keep the tremor from affecting her voice. "I agreed to fulfill this job. Please be excused. The baby and I are doing fine. Can't you see that you are . . . upsetting her?"

"We'll put the baby in her bed where all slobbering babies belong and have a little settling of matters," Jed said. "You were snatched away from me before, but you won't be this time. There'll be no heroic rescuer blundering from the bushes like there was at the well. Your gallant knight is not here today."

"I—I'm sure I don't know what you are talking about." Ellie's tight smile masked her irritation, her suffocating fright.

"Oh, I forgot. You pulled a faint on me before your champion showed up, didn't you? Well, I can tell you one thing, kitten, I sure didn't appreciate his nosy interference."

"Of whom are you speaking?"

"Your hired man, that's who!"

"Wayne? He came when I fainted?"

"In all his glory. He thinks he's tough."

Keep him talking . . . I've got to keep him talking! thought Ellie. *Talk about anything—divert him.*

But it didn't work.

"You're on *my* territory now! Here! Let me have that baby. I'll put her up myself." Jed grappled for the baby, but the child laid her head against Ellie, and when he tried to pull her away, she howled in frustration and protest.

"She doesn't want you," Ellie said.

"We don't care what she wants or doesn't want. It's what *I* want that matters. When I'm through with you, you won't be so pious or innocent!" A glassy wildness brightened his stony eyes.

Ellie lifted her chin. "You will *leave me alone!*"

"You'll do, kitten." He gave a shallow, sardonic laugh. "I like your fire, your vinegar. I've always wanted to capture a she-angel with buckskin—colored hair and dust her pretty wings with a bit of earth." He gave the baby a fierce yank, and Ellie, afraid the child would be pulled apart if she insisted on keeping her, turned loose. Jed thrust the child roughly into her crib, bringing out a loud, angry squawl. "Dumb kid," he spat. "I hate you!"

"Please don't hurt her," Ellie pled.

When he returned, he caught Ellie by the shoulders with such force that she winced. "Now see here, pet. I'll have a closer look at that buckskin mane." He moved his face close to hers and reached for her hair.

"No!" she screamed, trying to pull away.

Jed's mocking laugh had hardly left his throat when

Wayne stepped through the front door with a casual greeting, bearing an armload of firewood.

"Pardon me," Wayne said easily, his eyes following Jed as he jumped back, releasing Ellie. "I brought some wood. . . ."

"Sure." Jed stood sullenly waiting for Wayne to fill the woodbox and take his leave. "Saves me the trouble. I hate hauling wood. But we didn't need any more wood. We have plenty."

The baby continued to protest with loud cries. "Is the child all right?" Wayne looked at Ellie.

"I don't know, sir. I'll . . . go see." She slipped into the baby's room and did not return.

"You're free to go any time now." Jed narrowed his eyes. They glinted with malice. "This is my house, not yours."

"The *wings,* God," prayed Ellie frantically. "The wings of an eagle . . . Don't let Wayne leave now! Just for today . . . let him stay and be . . . the wings that save me. . . ."

"I believe I'll stay awhile, now that I'm here, and do a bit of repair work," Wayne said. "I told Mr. Greaves that I would help him get the old place shipshape. It's quite a job for one man you know. I understand you aren't talented for carpentry. But that's all right. I don't mind. I rather enjoy working with my hands. I never could abide a man with more dirt on his tongue than on his hands. I understand, too, that the old house hasn't been occupied for several years." Wayne talked in a pleasant, everyday manner.

He's driving Jed Greaves to madness, Ellie thought, hushing the child. *And he knows it.*

"You know, it's not good for a house to stand vacant," Wayne went on. "Sometimes rats move in uninvited."

"You . . . you . . ." Jed frothed.

"Did I say something I shouldn't have said?"

"Of all days, why do you have to work today?" Jed's voice hung somewhere between a question and a demand.

"Why, I thought it would be as good a time as any— with your folks gone for the day and all. The less people underfoot the better when one has inside repairs to make."

"Well, it ain't a good time. So scram!"

"I think I'll be the judge of when I do my extra jobs. Mr. Webster is away for the day, too, and I have a bit of time on my hands. I might be busy at something else tomorrow." Wayne crossed the room to examine a loose facing. "I'm sure glad I thought to bring along my hammer and some nails. Hammers are good for a lot of things. In houses like these, one might need to use a hammer to chase away a rat. . . ."

Jed stormed out in blind fury, muttering curses.

Wayne walked to the door of the nursery. For one long moment, he observed but said nothing. Then, through clenched teeth, he spoke in a gravelly voice, "You can take the baby back to the rocker if you'd like, miss. I . . . need to do some work in this room. It shouldn't take long. If the young man comes back to bother you, . . . let me know."

Wayne worked the day away in the house, saying nothing to Ellie. His whistling presence brought comfort, and Jed did not return.

When Ellie lay the child down for a nap, her eyes sought the heart on the wall that had caused her anguish.

It was gone. The whole thing had been scraped off, a victim of Wayne's "repairs." He must have sensed that she had rather it not be there at all than to have Daniel's expression of devotion defiled with Jed's substitution of initials. Daniel would have been grateful to Wayne for the favor.

Wayne had not been gone long when the Greaves returned. They were both in a foul mood. They snapped at each other. The pout on Mazie's oval face and Mr. Greaves' scowling made a duet of discord that filled the room with disharmony.

"Of all days for the land man to be away!" growled Mr. Greaves, rolling his complaint around a wad of chewing tobacco. "Away on some emergency. Bah! Them government agencies will tell you anything just so's they don't have to help a feller!"

"I can't understand, Greaves, why you couldn't get some kind of information on this property. Lawsy, what a waste of a day!"

"Just means another trip into town, Mazie."

She bunched her rounded shoulders. "Means you'll have to come again and keep Dee," she said to Ellie. "I wouldn't think of takin' 'er with me."

Ellie knew that she would never again agree to care for the beloved baby. Unless... That was an idea! Perhaps Mazie Greaves would bring the child to her home the next time.

Ellie left the feuding couple after kissing Dee's chubby hand. She filled her lungs with winter's pungent air, thankful to be headed for safety.

She didn't see Wayne. But she sensed that he kept her in sight all the way home to make sure no harm befell her. Harm named Jed.

CHAPTER FOURTEEN
Julius

The smell of freshly baked gingerbread permeated the whole house and wafted out to the front porch.

"Um-mmm! What is that heavenly smell?" The unfamiliar voice reached Ellie as she sat on the quilt-box lid turning collars on the boys' school shirts. She dropped the scissors. The voice was rich and deep.

"Something Eleanor is cooking, I wager." The unmistakable overtone came from Beatrice. "I told you she was no slouch for a cook. You should taste her berry pies! Come on in and meet her."

Ellie arose to make her escape, but not quite in time.

"Oh, there you are, Eleanor! I was hoping we wouldn't find you up to your elbows in soapsuds! My son, Julius, has come home with us for a visit. Julius, this is Eleanor Webster, Mr. Webster's only daughter."

Ellie looked up into laughing blue eyes, the bluest eyes she had ever seen. "Eleanor! I'm pleased to meet you, I'm sure." The man pretended to tip an invisible hat, bowing. "But may I *please* just call you Ellie?"

"Oh, for crying aloud, Julius," scolded Beatrice. "Why must you be so trying? Eleanor sounds so much more *refined*."

"She looks *fine* enough without being *re*fined by you, Beatrice." It sounded like a bad drama rehearsal with that irreverent line thrown in for a pun. Ellie liked it.

Ellie took in the masculine features. An antonym to his florid mother, Julius stood tall, trim, and confident. None of his mother's intimidations daunted him. Rather, he left one doubting that *anything* daunted him.

"*Trying* she says I am, Ellie. And she's quite right this once. Trying I am: trying to hold myself away from the wonderful cake that I smell. Beatrice never cooked anything that tempted me to pure robbery as that aroma does! Shall I yield, or shall I forbear?"

"*Please*, Julius." Gesturing despair, Beatrice covered her face with her hands. "Can't you mind your manners?"

Julius winked at Ellie, a slow, conspiratorial wink.

"Julius will be staying for a few days, Eleanor. I hope that you can abide him."

"I hope we can abide *her*." He spoke to Ellie, restructuring Beatrice's words and spreading out his hands palms up. "If *you'll* do the cooking, I might stay a year. However, if *Beatrice* does the honors, I may take my leave on the morrow."

"I normally don't compromise on work plans, Eleanor. But at the request of Julius, you may cook all the meals while he is here. One does like a new taste experience after a quarter of a century with the same cook."

Julius gave an exaggerated sigh. "Glory be!" he said. "My zodiac has rescued me! I won't have to abide her culinary artlessness."

Julius had a way of loosening the atmosphere. With him, nothing was serious or sacred. The charm of this son of Beatrice affected the whole of the Webster family. His lighthearted, almost flippant, outlook on life made the evening meals times of fun and fellowship. Walter and Willy giggled like girls at his jokes, providing him the audience he craved for his clowning. With his wit and humor, he succeeded in taking Ellie's mind from more melancholy thoughts. And the way he handled Beatrice seemed to her nothing short of a miracle. Beatrice was putty in his hands!

His familiarity—the winks, pats, and endearing names—were as much a part of his airy personality as his blue eyes were contributors to his good looks. Ellie learned to accept it when he called her "baby doll" and "honey." She even found that she liked his attention.

On several occasions, Wayne ate hurriedly and excused himself from the supper table on one ruse or another. Ellie couldn't decide whether he approved of Julius or not. But then why should it matter to her how Wayne felt about this visitor?

Julius was evidently quite at home, for he extended his stay into the second week. He said he wished to stay longer because he just couldn't leave "the delicious bread pudding." The announcement both pleased and flattered Ellie. Travis whispered to Ellie that he had invited Julius to stay "forever" so that she might go on cooking forever.

"I think you are spoiling Julius with your feed, Eleanor," Beatrice said. "He may just move in with us!" Certainly life with her stepmother was more endurable when Julius was there, Ellie decided. And her brothers enjoyed the entertainment of this self-made comedian.

Except for Wayne, everyone was happier.

One night, Julius asked Ellie to sit up with him after the others had gone to bed. He amused her with stories of his childhood, chock full of humor. He had a way of putting one at ease. She felt comfortable with him—almost like she had felt with Daniel. Only the depth was not there . . . yet.

The hour grew late, and still they chatted, forgetting the time.

Julius's question came unexpectedly. "You're such a brilliant girl, Ellie. And so very pretty. How is it that you've never been roped into marriage?"

Her face burned. "I had a . . . childhood sweetheart once. And I've never found anyone since. That is, I've never given anyone else a chance to . . . to steal my heart."

"And you never plan to?" Without warning, he placed his hand on hers. "I make a pretty good thief."

"I've . . . I've given it some consideration in the last few days." She made no effort to remove her hand.

Was it the wind, or did someone pass by the window?

"I've always wanted a wife who could make wonderful berry pie." He winked. Then he warbled "Can she make a berry pie, Billy Boy, Billy Boy?" in a high, silly falsetto. "Would you consider being my baker?"

"I really don't know much about you. . . ."

"I've always heard that it isn't the past that matters," he said. "It's the future that counts. One, two, three. I'm ready to start counting."

"I'll have to pray about it."

"Pray? Pray tell, why pray?"

"Oh, I just pray about everything!"

"But why?"

"God knows things that I don't know."

"But how could prayer help you to decide whether you should cook berry pie for me or for someone else? God leaves those decisions up to you."

"But God will help me to know. I can't tell you how I'll know, but I will."

"Well, if you must, pray."

"I must."

"How long will it take to know?"

"Probably not long."

It was past midnight when Ellie knelt beside her bed, careful not to awaken Walter and Willy with her prayers. Marrying Julius could be the perfect solution, her ticket away from Jed Greaves and Beatrice. Julius was personable; her father and brothers liked him. His irreverence would surely mellow with time and a Christian wife. Beatrice would be proud to introduce her as Julius's wife. Everyone would be pleased. Life would be more tolerable for her father if Beatrice had the run of the house. Beatrice could do things her way. And as for Wayne, his time of departure was at hand anyhow.

And if she married Julius and moved into town, there would be no more going to the well. She would be away from haunting memories. . . .

She burrowed into bed, dizzy with the unforeseen turn of events. The night held her in folds of uneasy sleep. She tossed her bed into a terrible disorder. Something was wrong. What could it be? The answer stepped almost within her reach; then it eluded her.

Neither Julius nor Beatrice showed up for breakfast. Ellie, her eyes badgered with dark circles from lack of rest, fed the schoolboys, her father, and Wayne. Wayne looked as though he had had no sleep himself.

When the dishes were cleared, Ellie pulled out her mending basket. She was in the middle of sewing a button on a shirt sleeve when she heard a noise like the tapping of tiny hooves running across the porch. The prancing stopped suddenly. It gave her such a strange sensation that she laid aside her needle and ran to the door.

She stood face to face with a girl about her own age but many steps up the social ladder from herself. Her grand dress of lavender taffeta rippled out in the back over a massive bustle. Up behind the wearer's small ears, a high collar fanned out above an inadequate shoulder stole. The finery spoke of a world unknown to Ellie. Frequent short looks kept her curiosity from becoming an open stare. But each time she glanced down, the magnet of girlish marvel brought her eyes back again. The young lady standing before her tapped little high-heeled shoes in a nervous staccato on the porch flooring.

In one swoop of a glance, and before a single word was spoken, Ellie anaylzed her. The lines about her painted lips told a story of spoiled dissatisfaction. The way she held her head revealed her poisonous pride. Selfishness spoke from her emerald green eyes, and her expensive dress exposed her desire for attention. Beneath it all, Ellie saw a shallow, unhappy woman, and she felt real pity for this poor rich girl, whoever she might be.

"Is this where the Websters live?" the lady asked, snappishly.

"Yes, it is. May I help you?"

"Is my mother-in-law here?"

"Your *mother-in-law?*"

"Beatrice Webster."

"I'm afraid I don't understand. I—I didn't know—that is, Beatrice never mentioned a daughter-in-law to me."

"Likely not. She hates me. She has done everything in her power to persuade her son to leave me since the day we married. Julius left about two weeks ago, and I know that Beatrice is at the root of it! I'm determined to find him and make him take care of me because I am his wife and I am with child!"

"Your husband is here."

"And *you* are trying to steal him from me!"

"I don't *want* your husband."

The girl stood in iron-faced silence.

Julius staggered into the sitting room, half asleep.

"My prayer was answered sooner than I thought, Julius," Ellie said evenly. "Your wife is here for you. And I think you'd best pack your things and go with her . . . *now.*"

CHAPTER FIFTEEN
The Revelation

*W*inter passed, as all time does, bringing sweet warmth to the earth's cold cheeks but doing nothing to unthaw the hoary frost of hopelessness that locked Ellie in its arctic grasp.

With the scheme for Julius aborted by Beatrice's despised daughter-in-law, Mrs. Webster became hostile toward Ellie. Apparently she felt that Ellie should have protected the secret of her son's whereabouts from his wife and joined the campaign to transfer him quietly from one marriage to another.

"Divorce is an acceptable policy nowadays, Eleanor," she said, her voice honed with condescension, "on grounds of incompatibility. And if ever two were incompatible, it is my son and his wife. She hies from a wealthy and snobbish family who silver-spooned her all her life. She won't lift a finger to do *anything,* and when Julius crosses her, she goes running home to her nanny. I tried to point all this out to him, but he listens like a deaf man.

"Now, it would be different with you and my Julius. If

you'll just wait until after this baby is born . . ." That's when Ellie left the room and refused to hear anything further that Beatrice had to say on the subject, further straining their relationship.

Beatrice took over the cooking of the main meal again with results as catastrophic as her first efforts. But the woman was stubborn. Her results became even more teeth defying, and Ellie suspected some spite was involved. The more the boys complained, the worse the food. They stuffed away an enormous breakfast—their salvation.

Nor did Beatrice's dislike for Wayne pass. Ellie sensed it in her attitude, saw it in her eyes when Wayne sat at the table, politely wordless. Somehow, in Beatrice's deluded mind, Wayne figured in the plot to destroy Julius's happiness, and she was determined to have him off the place as soon as possible.

In the interim between cold weather and hot, heavy black clouds emptied themselves without mercy on the land. Water crashed on the roof and slobbered over the window ledges in a cascade of small waterfalls. It seemed to Ellie that the heavens wept in her behalf since she hadn't enough tears to pay for all her heartaches. An ironic conceit on her part, perhaps, but the strange notion brought her a degree of comfort. Were the angels crying because God had somehow lost the pattern for her life?

When the rains subsided and the first robins appeared, pecking with their bobbing beaks on the pebble-strewn earth, Wayne began planting an enormous garden for the Webster family. Ellie had never seen such a garden. The few seeds that she hoarded, carefully guarding year after year, rested undisturbed in their crock jars pushed to the back of the pantry. Wayne went into town for new seeds, bringing back tomato slips and onion bulbs. He went into the woods and brought back blackberry vines, transplanting them in symmetrical hills of dirt in sight of the house.

He sowed a flower bed, too. Ellie watched out the window as the tall figure bent like a folding rule over the infant shoots, his gigantic hands patting earth about the new plants. He brought a cutting of a rose bush from somewhere and carefully set it out beside the porch. Observing him gave Ellie a tight feeling in her throat. This homeless man had a sort of soft hardness about him. Or was it a hard softness? Was the enamel on the inside or out? For what loved one had he heaped clay on a grave with those big, experienced hands?

Once, he lifted his scarred face and looked toward the house. Ellie moved away from the window.

Soon early jonquils bloomed with the throb of new life. They had been Daniel's favorite. The world changed to its dress of green. But none of the rejuvenating powers of spring took root in the soil of Ellie's worn-out heart this year. It was sealed in a tomb of perpetual winter and felt no tug to ever live again. What had she to live for except dreary hours that followed in the steps of other dreary hours? Wooden hearts didn't beat, she reminded herself.

Wayne would soon be gone, a victim of Beatrice's resentment. Ellie had begun to think of him as a sort of guardian angel shielding her from hardships, Jed Greaves, and perhaps even death itself. His quiet, faithful ministrations about the place brought a sense of security. When he was gone, she would feel a certain loss. What was life, though, but a succession of painful losses?

After school one lukewarm day, Travis found Ellie sweeping the splintery porch with her frayed straw broom. He shifted from one foot to another, a habit employed when he had something he wanted to discuss with her. She leaned on the worn broom handle and lifted her eyes in question. "You need to talk to me?"

"I got a question, Ellie."

"Say on."

"Why don't you like Jed Greaves?"

"*Jed?* He's . . . he's not my kind, Travis. He hasn't the stuff of a man in him."

"I know, Ellie. He's . . . wild. I don't like to be around him, an' I wish Jimmy wouldn't feather with 'im. I'm glad you don't like 'im. I hope you'll never change your mind."

"You need never worry, Travis."

"Then I got one more question."

"Yes?"

"Why don't you like Wayne?" Travis caught her by surprise. She didn't quite know what to say.

"Why, . . . I do," she stammered, embarrassed.

"I mean for a *beau,*" he clarified. "I heard Paw say you'll be twenty-two pretty soon. An' Beatrice says you'll soon be an *old maid.*" He spoke the words as if they might be a viper.

Ellie's hand fluttered to her throat. "I don't—*want* a beau. Is it so bad that I would want to stay here and care for my father and my brothers? And cook breakfast?"

"But can't you see that Wayne likes you special, Ellie?"

"Why, . . . no."

"Well, I can tell even if you can't! I think you must be blind. Look at all th' nice things he does for you. Look at the big garden he planted for you so you wouldn't have to get your hands dirty. And even flowers. Look at the blackberry plants he brought from the woods so's you wouldn't have to chance gettin' poison ivy pickin' berries for your pies. He milks th' cows an' gathers th' eggs an' goes to th' well for water an' brings up th' wood an'—"

"You could take a few lessons, Travis. He's a gentleman."

"Sure he's a gentleman, Ellie. A real honest-to-goodness one. I wish I could be half so good. You couldn't beat him nowhere. If I was a girl ripe for marryin', I tell you *I* wouldn't let him get away!"

"I'll never have another . . . sweetheart." Speaking the endearment hurt her mouth.

"You're . . . you're . . . Sometimes you're just plain *stupid*, Ellie. You ain't still hopin' on Daniel Brock, are you? Cause if you are, you can forget him. He's *dead*."

Travis's last word drove a dagger deep into Ellie's heart, leaving it torn and bleeding. The fatal word, said aloud and with such emphasis of finality, bruised worse than she imagined possible. She turned away so that her brother could not see the tears that budded behind her lids. Would the pain never end?

Travis stepped off the end of the porch and was gone. The retreat of his solid footsteps relieved Ellie of further conversation.

Ellie could not lift her eyes to meet Wayne's after the disclosure. She would not encourage any attention from him. She had promised to belong to Daniel Brock, and for her that promise seemed to reach past the grave into eternity. Even buried on a lonely desert somewhere, he would live on forever in her heart. And who knew but what he might be looking down from "Abraham's bosom" to the earth right now?

When Mr. Webster said that he planned to sell off some of the stock in the late spring and let Wayne go, Ellie felt relief. What if, in a moment of human weakness, she let her heart lean too far in the direction of this gentle stranger who had shown such unreserved kindness toward her? If Travis had never brought up the subject . . . never made the revelation . . . But he had. And now Ellie must put a legion of soldiers around her emotions to be on constant guard.

A shiver passed over her frail frame. When Wayne was gone, she would be compelled to go back to the well—back down the path that took her by the tree—her tree and Daniel's—with the beautiful heart carved deep in its body.

She would go on living with her wooden heart.

CHAPTER SIXTEEN

Teacher Conference

A rub board propped against the back of the house matched the galvanized washtub with its waterline ring. Fire crackled under the big, black iron pot. Monday was washday. Beatrice had three soiled items to everyone else's one.

Ellie sorted the clothes into piles according to color: whites, lights, darks. She always checked the boys' trousers with care before tossing them into the boiling water. Today was no exception.

A pocket of Jimmy's pants held a crumpled note from his schoolteacher warning that more absences from class would mean no promotion to a higher grade for the boy. The note suggested a conference with a family member. Jimmy had not mentioned the note. With it were a silver dollar and a ticket for a show.

Ellie's mouth went dry. What would her dear mother have done in this situation? This was the work of Jed, doubtless. Travis had mentioned Jimmy's too-close association with the neighbor boy. In Ellie's heart, she knew the money was ill-gotten. With a weary sigh, she placed the items into her apron pocket and finshed the day's wash.

Trouble had multiplied since the incorrigible young man named Jed Greaves moved next door. And the future promised no letup of evil's multiplication tables. What could she do?

Mr. Webster would be no help. Caught in the quicksands of problems of his own making—problems generated and perpetrated by Beatrice—he struggled with financial woes bordering on bankruptcy. Already, he planned to sell off some of the stock and had even mentioned forfeiting irreplaceable acreage to make ends meet. *To satisfy the whims of his spoiled wife.* Ellie thought bitterly. *Why should she be pampered and queened when my own mother worked so hard?*

What would she do about the note from the teacher? Any interaction would be up to her. Going to school for a conference was not a pleasant thought; she didn't know how she would manage it. But she had to try to salvage her brother for the sake of her beloved mother who lay at rest in the cemetery.

Ellie told Beatrice that she was going "for a walk" the next afternoon, and she set out on foot for the schoolhouse, timing her arrival to coincide with the dismissal of classes. She saw none of spring's preening colors as she hurried along. None of the wild cherry blossoms, the buttercups, or the honeysuckle. Her singular goal blotted up her attention. What could she say . . . do . . . when she got to the school?

She paused at the door of the box-shaped building. Mr. Samuelson, a thin, plain-faced man, nodded for her to come in as he pulled the bell rope to signal day's end for his restless students. They scattered in all directions with whoops and shouts, glad to be free.

Travis gave Ellie a puzzled look. "Is something wrong at home?" he asked.

"No. I just need to talk to the teacher about . . . about Jimmy."

"Yes, I think you do, Ellie. I'm worried 'bout him. He skipped school agin today. That's twice this week."

"Do you know where he is?"

"Somewhere with Jed, I 'spect."

"I'm not sure it will help to talk to the teacher."

"Naw, th' teacher can't do nuthin'. But your comin' will show we're concerned. That'll help. You want that I should wait on you an' walk home with you when you're finished, Ellie?"

"No. You go on with Walter and Willy. Don't say anything to Beatrice or Paw about my being here. I'll be home directly."

Mr. Samuelson removed his wire-rimmed monocle and pointed Ellie to a chair in front of his desk in an executive fashion. Ellie had not met this professor, who transferred out from Springdale when Ellie's teacher retired. Her teacher had been a woman, and Ellie wished for her friendly, elderly teacher today.

"I'm Emil Samuelson." He held out a bony hand. The handshake seemed an afterthought.

"Pleased to meet you, I'm sure," Ellie said, eager to drop the hand that held hers. It felt small and limp.

"Familial favor indicates that you are Miss Webster, older sibling of the truant Jimmy Webster." He talked in a recorded-cylinder voice. "Thank you for responding to my request for a conference. And with such haste. That reveals your manifest concern. You are aware of the circumstances under which I suggested this meeting?"

"I didn't know, sir, that Jimmy had been absenting himself from school until . . . until I found the note in his pocket on washday. That was yesterday. How long has this . . . this skipping school been going on?"

"With regret I inform you that Jimmy's marks have been declining all semester, Miss Webster. He seems to have lost interest in the pursuit of his education and has become delinquent in submitting his assignments. And that is truly lamentable."

"What would you suggest that I do, sir?"

"Are you the authoritarian of your family at this time?"

"The what?"

"The one who runs the family. The boss."

"Oh, no, sir. But I am the one who cares what happens to my brothers."

"I see." He toyed with the eyeglass. "Surely you have a father—mother?"

"My mother is deceased, and my father hasn't time for conferences. With a little begging from Jimmy, he might even let him quit school and help on the farm since our hired hand is leaving."

"How preposterous! You'll insist that Jimmy attend classes, please, Miss Webster. Life has become so complicated that one can hardly *breathe* without advanced education. How would one know if he were inhaling oxygen and exhaling carbon dioxide or vice versa without the scientific foundation to advise us?" His eyes, almond shaped and small, were accusing.

"I would like to see each of my brothers have the best education possible, sir," Ellie agreed.

"Ah, a perspicacious young lady, you are! Did you complete your own schooling?"

"I discontiued my schooling in ninth grade. I—lost interest."

"What a pity. Some time a loss of interest can be laid at the feet of the professor. This isn't the case with Jimmy, to be sure. But wait! I could tutor you yet. Why, you might wish someday to be a teacher. Or a bookkeeper. Or a bank teller. You've but started your life's journey—and life is a bumpy road without a proper education. We could meet here, say, one afternoon a week after my regular classes."

"I really don't think I would have time to—"

"And think! Your renewed interest in education would surely spark a fresh flame of interest in your recalcitrant brother! With a little push and pull, a bit of motivation, you could catch him up with his counterparts. I will help you, you will help him, and I will see that he is promoted in return."

"It seems—"

"What about Wednesday afternoons? That's a good midweek day. Any obligations that you might have at home could be scheduled before or after that median."

"I don't see that I need an education to wash clothes or to go to the well for water."

"But Miss Webster, that's *exactly* my point. You don't know what fate may have in her offing! You are much too young to develop an attitude of lassitude. Are you considering marriage?"

"No, sir."

"Then you need a career. At some strategic point in time, your father will die or become disabled, and your brothers will find their predetermined path in life. You cannot—may I stress you *must* not—neglect this great opportunity I am offering."

"What supplies would I need?"

"I'll furnish all the supplies. All you need bring is yourself and your intelligent, active mind!"

"I won't promise. But I will think about it."

"Please don't turn down such a proposal, Miss Webster. I'm making you an *extraordinary* offer."

Ellie started for home, her thoughts a whirlpool of confusion. What Mr. Samuelson had said made sense. If she never planned to marry, she should equip herself for a self-supporting role in life. Mr. Samuelson, this skinny man with his flat, gray eyes and sparse moustache, was trying to be helpful. Being an educator, his first and foremost thought was education. He couldn't be faulted for that.

Her mind went back to Jimmy. Truancy wasn't Jimmy's only problem. Jimmy was rebelling against his stepmother, against the loss of his father's attention. Jimmy's schooling was much more important than her own.

Probably no one could help Jimmy except Wayne. But Wayne would be leaving soon. For her own sake, it mattered not. But she dreaded Wayne's departure for Jimmy's sake. She had hoped that Wayne could help in setting Jimmy back on the proper track before he left. Jed seemed to fear no one except Wayne. With Wayne gone, Ellie feared that Jed would make himself at home on the Webster property. It would be a source of agitation to her as well as a spiritual pitfall for Jimmy. Her head swam

in the pool of problems.
Flying hooves came around the corner behind her. She jumped to one side of the one-lane road just in time to keep herself from being overrun. Jed Greaves and Jimmy whipped by, riding double and laughing riotously. She got a whiff of something.
Whiskey! The boys had been drinking!

CHAPTER SEVENTEEN
The Ultimatum

"*E*leanor, I need to speak with you." Beatrice's face bode no good.

"Yes, ma'am."

"There seems to be some underhandedness going on in this household, and you seem to be at the taproot."

"I'm afraid I don't know what you are talking about."

"I'm afraid that you do."

"Pardon me if I must persist, Beatrice, but I don't." With concentrated effort, Ellie controlled her voice, keeping it low and balanced.

"I found a stash of biscuits in Travis's and Jimmy's room. And they weren't biscuits that *I* made but biscuits that *you* made. Have you an explanation for that?"

"I suppose the boys were hungry."

"You will not be impudent, Eleanor."

"No offense meant, ma'am. I know of no reason other than hunger that would call for taking food into one's room."

"There is no call for them being hungry. I cook

generous portions of food each evening. The bread *I* make is often untouched."

"I'll be glad to make the bread for you if you'd like."

"You are missing the point entirely. The point is that you are working against the family unity in a secret and destructive way. If the boys are hiding your bread in their room to boycott my own—which is apparently just what they are trying to do—I shall hold you accountable.

"And there's another skeleton I've found hiding in the closet. It appears that at some time or other you have kept the hired hand in the house without our knowledge. I asked your father about it, and he knew nothing. But I know, because while cleaning the attic room, I found a scrap of a message he had directed to you."

"To me? You must be mistaken."

"Oh, no. I have the proof right here." She patted a ragged piece of paper, dirtied with fingerprints. "You haven't satisfied my question. When did you let the man lodge in our attic?"

"Back during the winter snowstorm."

"And you tried to hide it from your father and me?"

"I beg to disagree. I didn't try to hide anything from anyone. The boys were afraid Wayne might freeze to death in the old barn. They asked if he might bring his bedroll and sleep in the attic."

"The boys . . . the boys . . . What an excuse! For shame that a big girl like you would throw off on her younger brothers to escape censure. You can't fool me. *I* know what girls do when nobody is around to supervise them."

"Stop!" Ellie's eyes flashed. "I won't hear it! Ask any of my brothers how I conducted myself while Wayne was in the house. We made candy and snow ice cream and read the Bible—."

"Miss *Pious!*" scorned Beatrice. "Ask your brothers indeed! Any one of them would lie for you at the drop of a hatpin. I know about brothers, too. Julius covered for Wancille—"

"Your own children may have been dishonest and immoral," Ellie flung angrily, "but you will not put the Websters in the category with them. I have nothing to hide and no shame to cover."

"Then read this!" Beatrice thrust the torn note sheet toward Ellie, and she opened it with fingers that shook from sheer anger. The message, with its poorly written characters, might have been printed by a first grader.

"Dear Ellie," it began. "I would like to talk to you alone. There are some things I need to explain. I'll always love you—" The rest of the page was torn away.

"There!" gloated Beatrice. "I've tried to convince your father that there was something between you and that unsightly man since the day I arrived."

"I know nothing about it. Wayne never gave that letter to me or any other letter."

"You are a convincing liar, Eleanor. But a liar nonetheless."

"I repeat: there is nothing between Wayne and me, Beatrice." She set her mouth, suggesting an end to the discussion.

The letter probably wasn't written by Wayne at all, she concluded. The handwriting didn't match his personality. More likely, Jed had written the note and Wayne had intercepted it. But Beatrice would understand none of this. Her opinionated mind grasped only what it wished.

It was evident that Beatrice did not believe her, so why bother to be defensive?

"And last, but not least, is the disrespect you are sowing in Jimmy's heart for me. You are working diametrically against the family's harmony. I've spoken to your father a hundred times about it, and he refuses to give you an ultimatum. When it comes to his children, your father is a spineless wimp. So the nasty job falls to me.

"I cannot continue living in this house with *you* bringing strife and discord. So either *I* go, or *you* go. I had hoped it would never come to this. You were so agreeable at the start. But most stepchildren try to make a good first impression. That's the kind to watch. I want you to know, though, that if I should be forced to divorce your father, I shall advertise that *you* put the wedge between us."

"You married my father. This is your home. I will go." Ellie's tongue spoke on its own.

"Now, I won't put you into the woods to starve, of course. I have a big, generous heart. I might be able to persuade Wancille to take you in. At least temporarily, until you can get a job and a place of your own."

"No, thank you. I'll find some place."

Ellie said no more. Her future loomed too dark for rational thought. Where would she go? What would she do? Whatever the cost to herself, she must not bring scandal to her father's honorable name. Her father a divorced man? Never!

"Have you any immediate plans?"

"I . . . I had planned to . . . that is, Mr. Samuelson promised to tutor me so that I might receive my diploma. If I might have a few days, just until school is out, at least to brush up on my education, I think I can be ready to earn my wage."

"Why, certainly, Eleanor." Beatrice switched from a lion to a lamb. "I had no idea you were doing *anything* to prepare yourself to be self-supporting. I just assumed that your father would be saddled with your care forever. If dear Mr. Samuelson is willing to work with you, I'm in absolute agreement. That's so very generous of him, to be sure. He's such a delightful, wonderful man. He wanted to court my Wancille, but he's much too slow for her. She likes *dashing* men. But she could have considered Mr. Samuelson's money. If he'd had just a bit more, that is."

"If I may be excused, I need to gather the clothes from the lines before dark." Ellie fled the house.

Travis found her at the clothesline crying. "What is it, Ellie? Is that old hag badgerin' you again?"

"She is determined that there is something going on between Wayne and me."

"I wish there was."

"Do you know anything about this note, Travis?" She slipped the portion of letter, forgotten by Beatrice, from her pocket. "Beatrice found it in the attic, and she says that Wayne wrote it."

Travis examined the scrap of paper. "That's not Wayne's writin', Ellie."

"And . . . and I need to leave here, Travis. Beatrice blames me for . . . for Jimmy's rebellion. She says I'm working against her."

"Someone needs to work against *her*."

"If I don't move, she'll move out on Paw."

"Let 'er move. Good riddance."

"It wouldn't be proper, Travis. I can't bear to think of Paw's good name being smeared in a divorce court. Beatrice would probably see that it got in the newspaper! What—what would our mother do if she knew? Oh, Travis!"

"Now you can just quit your worryin', Ellie. I don't know much about prayer. But Wayne has been teachin' me. Every evenin' we meet in th' loft of th' barn. He has made us what he calls an 'altar' there. We have a whole lot of things we're prayin' about. One of them is Jimmy. And another is you."

"You and Wayne are praying for me?"

"We never miss a day. And we're prayin' for Beatrice, too. Wayne said God wants us to pray for our enemies— those who despitefully use us. We pray for her ever' day, too. Wayne says he thinks that's why she is so miserable —because she's fightin' against God."

"But Wayne will be leaving in just a few days."

"Yeah, but I don't spect God is goin' anywhere, Ellie."

CHAPTER EIGHTEEN

The Rosebud

Plink . . . plink . . . plink-plink . . . The early English peas hit the bottom of the dishpan in a noisy, rhythmic pattern. Ellie paused to straighten her back, casting a fixed look into the woods teeming with new life but seeing none of it. On the clothesline hung the cheesecloth bags, dripping with wet, milky whey. When all the moisture seeped out, the clabbered milk would be crumbly cottage cheese. She would miss all this when she had to leave the farm.

A movement, something picking its way through the bushes, caught her attention. It broke into the clearing. Mazie Greaves!

She plodded to the house in her usual huff-and-puff manner, dropping with a heavy plunge to the porch floor. "Whew! It's getting warm! I ain't much on hot weather."

"I'm afraid it will get warmer."

"I see you are shellin' your peas. I tried to get Jeddy to pick mine for me this mornin', but he ran off to town again. It's just as well he didn't pick 'um, though, 'cause

I wouldn't 've had time to shell 'um today."

"Ummmm." Ellie kept working.

"D'ya know what I think? I think Jeddy's got a woman friend in town. He usually has several scattered around. I hope you don't mind, Ellie. That's just Jeddy."

"Me? Mind? What difference could it make to me, Mrs. Greaves?"

"Why, Jeddy said you was sweet on him. He said he might marry you."

"Oh, no, Mrs. Greaves! Jed is very mistaken. Pardon me, but he is not at all my type. I could never consider him even a close friend."

"I don't blame you, Ellie. And, lawsy, I'm glad. You're too white-hearted for Jed...." She hurried on. "I haven't much time. I left the baby by 'erself. She's asleep. Course, Greaves is just outside hitchin' up th' wagon. He could hear her if'n she cried, but I don't know that he'd do a blessed thing about it. I need you to come right over an' watch her while we go into town. Nobody answered th' notice th' land man put in th' paper about th' property, so we can start drawing up a new deed or whatever they do—"

Beatrice opened the door and stepped onto the porch. A look of amused interest showed on her sleep-swollen face.

"You must be Miz Webster." A stranger didn't stay a stranger to Mazie. "I'm Mazie Greaves, old man Greaves's woman. Your neighbor over. Beggin' pardon for not comin' to greet you sooner, but I'm stuck with a baby to tend. And that's why I'm here: to ask your daughter to see after my kid while th' old man an' me buggy into town on business."

"But . . ." Ellie tried to cut in to her conversation, without success.

"The business being our land over there." She flapped her hand in the direction of the Brock property. "I'm a'ready sick of th' stupid place. It *crawls* with black spiders! Now I wisht I'd married th' boy that I dumped for old man Greaves! He may have been irresponsible, but he was a romeo! My mother warned me not to marry Greaves; she said he was too old for me, but you know how headstrong girls can be."

"Yes, I know." Beatrice nodded toward Ellie.

"And I was one of them headstrong kind. But I've got to hurry right back now. You can come right along with me, Ellie."

"I'm sorry, Mrs. Greaves, but I won't be able to keep your baby in your home this time."

"Eleanor!" rebuked Beatrice. "You will not be impolite. I would have thought your mother taught you better. Of course, you will go along with our new neighbor and keep her children."

"I only have one child, Miz Webster," corrected Mazie. "Lawsy! One's aplenty!"

Ellie turned to Mazie. "I will be delighted to keep your baby here in my own home, but I cannot come to your house again, for reasons I don't care to disclose."

"Oh, don't be pettish, Eleanor," scolded Beatrice. "One place is as good as the other. What matters where you keep the child?"

"It's Jeddy, I know, Miz Webster," supplied Mazie. "He told me that he dropped in just to tease Ellie when she was there before. Jed likes funnin'. Course, he wouldn't hurt a flea! He just *will* torment girls, though."

She turned to Ellie. "But I told you he ran off to town—"

Ellie shook her head. "I will keep your baby here, Mrs. Greaves, and nowhere else." Her tone left no room for compromise.

"See. Eleanor can be stubborn." Beatrice gave an indifferent yawn.

"Well, Greaves will be plenty angry with me, but I'll have him drop by here as we go to town and leave Dee." She hustled off, taking the same shortcut through the brush by which she came.

It was a bad day. The feverish baby fretted constantly. In spite of all Ellie's efforts at rocking, walking, and bouncing, the child whimpered and cried.

Beatrice, at tether's end and devoid of patience with children of any age, screamed at Ellie, making the baby more jittery. "Can't you make that brat shut up? If you can't quiet her, you can take her right over to her own house. She's giving me a headache."

Finally, Ellie took the child outside to pacify Beatrice. But the wind was too high for the comfort of the baby's ears. So Ellie sought the shelter of the barn. The lopsided structure was highroofed and cool. It smelled of old leather and sweet clover.

She had forgotten that this was Wayne's "house." When he climbed down the ladder from the hayloft, she made profuse apologies for her forgetfulness. "So thoughtless of me," she stammered.

"Please say no more." He brushed her chagrin aside. "You're always welcome in my humble abode. And what have we here?" He nodded toward the child.

"This is Mrs. Greaves's baby that I'm caring for. And she is ill today. She got on Beatrice's nerves so badly that

I—I was trying to find a place to keep her away from the house."

"*Mi casa es su casa,*" Wayne quoted with a flourish of his hand and a bow that bent him in the middle. Ellie gave him a quizzical look. He laughed. "That means 'My house is your house.' It's Spanish."

"Do you speak Spanish?"

"Not much. I learned a little in my travels. Say, this is the same baby you were keeping when I came to repair the Greaveses' house, isn't it?"

"Yes."

"I think if I were you, I'd be tempted to kidnap her. Isn't she a dandy?" He reached out to stroke her hair, and she stopped her crying to look at him with large, tear-filled eyes. "I hope I don't frighten her with this terrible face of mine." As if the child understood what he said, she gave him a blubbery, cooing smile.

"Ah, she just stole my heart!" He grinned.

"Mr. and Mrs. Greaves went into town to try to draw up some papers on the Brock land. No one showed up to oppose their taking it over. Of course, we . . . we knew they wouldn't be back after you told us what you did about the Brocks' . . . misfortune."

Wayne changed the subject that could only hurt Ellie. "That baby's face is so flushed that she must have some fever."

"I think she does. I haven't much experience with tending babies, I'm afraid."

"Let me look in her mouth." Very gently, he pried her mouth open. "Open up for Da—" he stopped, flustered, and then covered his discomposure by adding quickly, "That's right; open up, honey. Let me see your toofies."

He nodded. "Yep, just as I thought. She has a tooth almost through. She's teething. Her gums are pretty swollen. What I need to do is get a little ice from the icehouse and put it in a rag for her to bite down on. That will give her some relief." He acted glad to hurry away.
He's had a child of his own, Ellie thought. *He started to say "Daddy," and caught himself. It embarrassed him. He doesn't want me to know. But he cares too much. . . .*

The ice relieved the child's discomfort, and she fell into a fitful sleep.

"Just keep her here in *mi casa* as long as you wish," Wayne said. "Remember it's *su casa*. I have some work to do myself." He left without looking back. Did Ellie imagine it, or was there a tear in his one good eye?

Mazie Greaves came for the baby in the early afternoon. In her hand she held a rosebud just ready to burst into bloom. "This is my first rose on the bush closest to the house," she said. "Ain't got no money to pay you for your trouble, but I brung ya a flow'r." She took the baby and handed the rose to Ellie.

Unbidden tears leaped into Ellie's eyes, making her vision fuzzy. "Th-thank you."

"And looks like we got the papers signed. Leastwise, I won't have to go back anymore. Greaves is real tickled that things is goin' so well for us. We just lucked out, gettin' somebody's land that don't never intend on comin' back. They probably found 'um a better place."

"Yes, I'm . . . I'm sure they are in a better place." Ellie's voice was barely audible.

As soon as Mazie was gone, she fled to the barn before more tears brought questions from Beatrice.

A replica of the many beautiful roses Daniel had

brought to her, the parable it bore to her own life wrenched her heart. Just as her love, and Daniel's, began to unfold, it was nipped in the bud.

She found a fruit jar and walked to the well, willingly this time, to get water for this tribute to her dream. By the tree she stopped. "Daniel," she whispered as her fingers slid over the heart-shaped carving like a blind person reading Braille, "our love was just a bud—like this one—but it was beautiful."

She took the rose to the barn and left it there for fear that its presence in the house would bring tears at the most inopportune time.

Beatrice had a "sick headache" and insisted that Ellie prepare the evening meal. The boys and Wayne would be elated.

But Wayne did not come for supper.

CHAPTER NINETEEN

A Way Out

Ellie asked Mr. Samuelson if she might come for tutoring twice a week instead of just once a week. She thought the gleam in his near-sighted eyes indicated his joy of teaching.

"Ah, Miss Webster, what a delight to find such an apt scholar," he beamed. "Of course, you may come more often. Come as often as you wish!"

"I find that I must prepare myself to earn my own living sooner than I thought, so I need to learn all I can as quickly as possible," she told him.

Mr. Samuelson stroked his wiry little mostache. "Well, well, so in what locale will this employ situate you?"

She hadn't meant to get into a personal discussion. "I'll look for work in Springdale."

"Oh, no! No! Not until you have completed your education! And that could necessitate a year of thorough study. You can't work at a *common* job, Miss Webster. Why, your scrupulous father wouldn't hear to it—and neither would I! That would be *scandalous!*"

"If I cannot complete my courses here, I'll try to find a family that will give me room and board in exchange for cooking and housework. An elderly couple, perhaps. Or a widow."

"A maid? Oh, Miss Webster, never! Pray stay with me until I have groomed you for a well-paying, prestigious job with an attorney or a doctor or a financial institution."

"I'm afraid I haven't the time, Mr. Samuelson."

"What could be so pressing?"

Ellie swallowed hard. "My stepmother and I are at odds, sir. I have until school is dismissed for the summer to find another place to live. My presence in the home is . . . abrasive."

"Tut, tut. Now my understanding is enlightened. I can well comprehend your dilemma. But there are always resolutions to such perplexities. I'm sure I can help to guide your contemplation to some viable conclusion. In such an emotional upheaval as you find yourself, one sometimes is at variance with oneself and cannot properly classify one's credits and debits. Let's survey the options in your case."

"I have no options."

"Oh, don't capitulate to passiveness! One *always* has options, my dear. As long as there is human existence, there are options, as one of my old professors was wont to dictate. I think I could propose a way that you might continue your education *and* have a means of support concurrently."

"That would be nice, but I see no way."

"Now there you go, taking the passive route again. Lend your mental capacities to active, optimistic efforts."

"What would you suggest, Mr. Samuelson?"

"I will support you myself—"

"Oh, no, Mr. Samuelson! I absolutely would not allow it. Nor would my father!" Ellie recoiled, pushing back her chair in alarm.

"I'm not asking for charity."

"Charity it would not be. Charity is not what I am offering. Miss Webster, you haven't heard me to my conclusion. I am financially stable. Most people would call me wealthy. Why, then, you may query, my necessity of teaching? I teach because I *love* teaching, *not* for the pittance of remuneration that the state pays. I have a large, comfortable cottage, well furnished. I live alone, my family having preceded me in death. I do have one servant and one gardener. I am prepared to offer you a permanent home—"

"I cannot accept your offer, sir. It is unthinkable."

"You do comprehend that I am proposing marriage, of course?"

"That is even more unthinkable. It is unlikely that I shall ever marry. I have no plans of doing so."

"Have you specific reasons for your singular state in life, Miss Webster? Has this decision culminated from some tragedy, some fear?"

"I could not marry you because I don't love you."

The undaunted schoolteacher smiled a pleasant smile. "Of course, you do not. I am not asking you to love me—now or ever. I do not even want you to try. I do not love you, either."

"Then, why—?"

"What I am offering you is simply a marriage of convenience. Such a marriage is more popular nowadays than you realize. The problem is this: you need a residence. I need a companion. Someone to keep me company. You would continue your education, pursue a career if you choose. In fact, you would be unfettered, free to do whatever you please in life. We would both benefit, keeping our individuality, neither asking of the other what the other did not wish to contribute. I would provide for you well in exchange for your companionship—and for a berry pie now and then if you felt impelled to accommodate me in that particular manner."

"But, sir, I cannot imagine a marriage without love. That's what a union is all about."

"Love is a relative word, Miss Webster. A figment of one's imagination, if you will. There is really no such thing as love. Romance, maybe; love, no. I dare say you feigned yourself to be in love once."

"I was in love!"

"You were young, were you not?"

"Sixteen."

"My point exactly. I thought I was in that state of affairs, too. I was a mere twenty. But it was nothing more than a deep impression, an infatuation. It's mind over matter. A dream, not a reality. In our relationship, you wouldn't have to worry about whether you were in love or not. If you wished to pretend you were, fine. If in your honest search you found no affection there, that would be fine, too. If I have a love, it is for teaching. Teaching is my life, now and for always. That's likely why I've had no nuptials already; no one can accept my philosophy. But it makes so much sense.

"I would both respect you as my wife and show you unmitigated kindness in conjunction with the meeting of all your personal needs. I promise that you would lack for nothing in my care.

"In actuality, the highest echelon of all development is a dedication in which humanity can peacefully co-exist outside the arena of emotion. Emotional involvement is the cause of hurts, pain. Remove that, and you have none. What would it be like, Miss Webster, to live a life free from hurting? Don't you concur that there can be no hurting where there is no emotion? Can you comprehend that?" He blinked his eyes with a dull sort of excitement.

"And consider that I am considerably older than yourself—possibly twice your age. I have no living heirs. All that I have would become yours at my decease. I would leave you comfortably situated for life. Now, *that* is my definition of affection."

"I'm afraid I could never consider marriage under those circumstances."

"I know that it sounds incongruous to you right now. I anticipated that; I would have been disappointed if you had accepted my proposal at face value only. You've just been introduced to a new value system. But when you consider it from all angles, it will become an enticing offer, a brilliant alternative to making your own living as a common laborer.

"And you might consider that my career is local. You would be in close proximity with your father, your brothers, your homestead. You might wish to take your younger brothers into our home—in the event your stepmother gets at odds with them, too—to finish rearing. I would be content to educate them, even furnishing them with college tuition. My home is quite large enough to accommodate all of us. You might even wish to adopt a child. That would be entirely up to you. Whatever charitable undertakings you choose to negotiate in life will evoke no objections from me."

"I'd have to think about it."

"Most certainly. I wouldn't want you to be coerced into anything. Take as much time as you wish. And remember, my proposal is merely a suggestion. I would never impose even a friendship upon you, Miss Webster. It just seems to me that this is the logical way out for you. And for me.

"I'll be glad to give you a tour of my house anytime, and if it doesn't suit you, we will build to your specifications wherever you wish within my school district." The slow monotony of his words made Ellie think of a rundown phonograph that needed cranking.

"I would not think it necessary to have an elaborate or romantic wedding. That would be hypocritical, a strain on both of us. A civil ceremony would satisfy, with only the required witnesses. The less celebration, the better. We would want the change to be as devoid of trauma as possible so that our lives would progress as nearly as they are now."

Ellie grew tired of his wordiness. He must have sensed it; he sped up his phonograph voice to a faster pace, a higher pitch.

"If you wish to decline my offer, neither of us will be the worse. We'll simply forget that I mentioned it, and I will tutor you to the best of my ability until you go out into a competitive world to earn your wage as best you can. And now, may we resume our assignment, please, Miss Webster?"

Ellie walked home, lost in her own meditation. Mr. Samuelson's philosophy wrapped its dangerous tentacles around her conscience. If she never planned to find love again—and she didn't—then what could be so wrong with an arrangement that would give her financial security and guarantee her a home? In the opinion of most people, she would be marrying well. Beatrice and her father were sure to approve. She would be in a position to help her brothers. Such a marriage would solve many of her problems.

What negative results could the union create? She could think of none. Mr. Samuelson had plugged any leaking arguments she might have. In a marriage of convenience, she could still cling to her memories. Every year, they would grow more legendary as her hair turned to snowy white and her eyes dimmed. She would still be able to live with her wooden heart.

Emil and Ellie Samuelson. That didn't sound bad. It sounded much better than *Mr. and Mrs.* Samuelson. That *Mrs.* was reserved. It would always be reserved in her heart for *Mrs. Daniel Brock.* She had written it hundreds of times.

She stumbled on a rock and almost lost her balance. Was she losing her balance inside, too? What had Mr. Samuelson said about love? *There is really no such thing as love.*

With that statement she would have to disagree.

CHAPTER TWENTY
The Teacher's Call

Beatrice was still "puny" the next day, she said, and would Ellie please cook supper again?

Ellie put what heart she had into the planning and preparation of the meal. The garden yielded its scant first-fruits, but it was enough. Her menu included marble-sized potatoes that swam in a rich, buttery sauce and tender green beans small enough to cook whole. She had searched the woods' edge until she found enough wild boysenberries for a pie. Blackberry was Travis's favorite, but Willy preferred the boysenberry.

She wore Mr. Samuelson's proposal threadbare by turning it over and over in her mind. Would it be a wise choice or simply the way of least resistance for a tired soul and body? She had to think long-range. If she should decline this once-in-a-lifetime offer, her welfare would be in her own hands henceforth. And what if she should become ill? Who would care for her then? How would she sustain herself? Women weren't as physically strong as men. Mr. Samuelson's job was secure. And if he spoke the truth, he was financially at ease if he never worked another day in his life.

An extra voice, new but somehow familiar, came through the front door with Mr. Webster for the evening meal.

"The very aroma drives my olfactory senses to ravenous hunger, Mr. Webster. Thank you for the generosity of your invitation to participate in the repast."

The vocabulary could be none other than Mr. Samuelson's. Why had he come to see her father? And why should she be so annoyed that he did?

Beatrice ate a behemoth's amount of the tasty food in spite of her purposed illness. The presence of the schoolteacher loosened her tongue. She chauffeured most of the conversation, taking the verbal reins in her own hands.

"This confectionary creation is absolutely superb," Mr. Samuelson commented on the pie. "Did you make it, too, Mrs. Webster?" Obviously, he thought that Beatrice had cooked the meal. Willy jabbed Walter, causing the youngest Webster to choke on a suppressed giggle.

"No, Emil, Eleanor made the pie. That's one thing she *can* do better than my Wancille. Wancille is better at ices and beverages, though. Wancille can make wonderful crepes and souffles, too."

"Eleanor?"

"My stepdaughter here." She nodded toward Ellie.

"Oh, I wasn't apprised of the fact that her name was Eleanor. But I am pleased beyond measure, to be sure. Eleanor sounds much more distinguished than Ellie. Don't you concur with that, Mr. Webster?"

Mr. Webster hesitated. "Well, Ronald, answer the gentleman!" chided Beatrice. "I believe he asked you a question."

Caught in their web, Mr. Webster struggled. "I rather like Ellie myself," he said, turning red. "That's what her . . . mother named her."

"What is your preference, Miss Webster?" asked Mr. Samuelson.

Ellie started to answer when Beatrice closed her off with, "Oh, how should a girl who has never been introduced to society know what sounds best, Emil? We—you and I—shall call her Eleanor." She changed the subject abruptly. "We are so glad you have come. Like Shakespeare said, 'Eat, drink, and be merry. . . .' I like Shakespeare, don't you?"

"Yes, quite."

"And when was the last time you saw my Wancille, Emil?"

Mr. Samuelson gave an uneasy cough. "Ah, I can't just recall, Mrs. Webster."

"Was she doing well at your last encounter?"

Mr. Samuelson laughed, a grating, superficial laugh. "My dear Mrs. Webster! Your Wancille is *always* doing well for herself. I've never witnessed her in any other state of affairs."

"Will you be seeing her again in the near future?"

He gave Ellie a sharp, sidewise glance. "I have other engagements that are—ah—pending."

Beatrice frowned, her black eyebrows drawn up like two angry centipedes facing each other for duel. "I can't imagine any engagement so pressing as to keep you from dropping by for a soda with Wancille," she recountered.

When Mr. Samuelson had finished his pie, he pushed back his plate. "Very delicious, Eleanor," he said, dusting his moustache with his napkin. He turned to Mr. Webster.

"Sir," he said, "if you would be so accommodating as to dismiss everyone except your wife and daughter, I would like a private consultation with the three of you." Beatrice's expression was full of questions, and Ellie heard Walter's too-loud whisper as he exited. "Oh, no! Jimmy's probably in trouble with the teacher again." But Mr. Samuelson's mission had nothing to do with Jimmy. When the room was cleared of listening ears, he began, "I have proposed, sir, that your daughter become my wife." Ellie's skin prickled, seesawing from a hot sensation to a cold one.

Shock widened Mr. Webster's eyes. "Why, how thoughty of you, Mr. Samuelson. I mean, if that's what you and Ellie wish, of course. We'd been hoping she would . . . that is, we feel she'll never be happy until she has her own home."

Ellie noticed something stronger than shock settling in Beatrice's burning eyes.

"I'm prepared to take care of the young lady and provide the greatest comforts available," he continued. "I was left with a sizable inheritance. I am now probably the wealthiest man in the county."

Beatrice gave a perceptible gasp.

"As I told Ellie—excuse me—" his look just touched Beatrice, not staying long enough to perceive her dismay, *"Eleanor,* I teach because I have a profound love of imparting knowledge to the less knowledgeable. Not for the pitiful wage the state offers. I would scoff at their efforts to hire me if I were working for pay. Eleanor will not be bothered with financial woes, now or ever. My assets are open for Eleanor's examination if you doubt my credibility."

The lid of Beatrice's anger flew off. "So this is the explanation of *classes* you were being tutored in, is it, Eleanor?" She had a poisonous set to her dyed lips. "I should have known. You have deceived me at every turn—"

"No, Mrs. Webster," Mr. Samuelson defended, unruffled by her outburst. "I beg to contradict you in this instance. Indeed, Eleanor knew nothing of the plan until yesterday when I proposed to her. It took her quite by surprise. She informed me that she would, of necessity, curtail her education in a few days, so I discreetly inquired as to her future stratagem. She tells me she will be making her own wage, and rather than send her into the field of employment unprepared—"

"I don't understand what you are saying about Ellie's employment...." Mr. Webster held up his hand for attention, but Beatrice took over.

"I told you, Eleanor," little points of light glinted in Beatrice's stormy eyes, "that you were free to stay here until you *completed* your education. Emil, you are not to feel *obligated* to marry Eleanor. It's not as if I'm *putting her out*...."

"I should say not!" interjected Mr. Webster.

"Wancille would be most unhappy with me if she felt I pushed out an unwanted burden on you for my own convenience...."

"Oh, you have misunderstood, to be sure, Mrs. Webster," Mr. Samuelson hurried to explain. "It is my own decision to provide in an ample manner for Eleanor. Eleanor is really quite lovely. And anyone who can make such heavenly pies could never prove a burden, would you think?" He turned back to Mr. Webster, leaving Beatrice to seethe. "And, sir, Eleanor may spend as much time with her family as she wishes. Nothing will change, really. I only regret that I did not sense the availability of the neighboring property. I would certainly have purhased it myself—for Eleanor. Such appreciable acreage! Have you seen the rosebushes on that place? I plan to ask the new owner for a cutting for Eleanor...." He stopped, realizing that he was rambling. "Well, what do you think of my proposal, Mr. Webster? Does it meet with your approval?"

"Ellie is of age, and whomever she chooses to marry will have my blessings," Mr. Webster answered, still looking bewildered. "As for me, Mr. Samuelson, I would be pleased and proud to have you for a son-in-law."

"And you, Mrs. Webster?" Mr. Samuelson gave her a counterfeit smile.

"I would be pleased to have you for *my* son-in-law." Her eyes were flinty.

CHAPTER TWENTY-ONE

A Trip to Town

By Saturday, Beatrice felt no better. Her health, as well as her disposition, went down hill after Mr. Samuelson's visit. Only with determined effort was she able to be civil to anyone.

"You will have to go into town to the drugstore for bitters, I'm afraid, Ronald," she whined. "I'm getting much worse."

"I can't go today, Beatrice," Mr. Webster apologized. "I have a cow on the brink of calving. I can't afford to lose an animal with our finances as tight as they have been lately."

"Cows have had their calves without human help for a million years, Ronald. Imagine, putting an animal before your own wife!"

"It seems to me anyone could pick up the bitters for you, Beatrice. I'll send one of the boys."

"Oh, no! No! The boys are much too irresponsible to trust with medicine. I sent Jimmy for saleratus once, and he came back with salts!"

"They've never failed to bring back what I sent them for."

"And besides the medicine, Ronald, I need to get a letter to my daughter," she said. "It is a bit of an emergency. I need to let Wancille know just how sick I am. Why, if anything happened to me and she didn't even know that I was ill . . . oh, Ronald, you just *must* go!"

He sighed. "All right. I'll go."

Ellie heard the conversation. Peace was a high-priced commodity for her father, but it seemed he would pay to the last penny. She followed him outside. "I'll go to town in your place, Paw," she offered. "I know how much the livestock means to you. One of the boys can drive me in the buggy."

How long had it been since she had been to Springdale? A very long time. A sudden desire seized her, a desire to see what the town was like, how it had grown. It would be a good opportunity for self-evaluation, a chance to determine if she could cope in such an environment in the event she decided to decline Mr. Samuelson's offer of a loveless marriage of convenience.

She didn't see Wayne until he spoke. "Do you need a ride into town, Miss Webster? I've a bit of business there myself. I'll be glad for you to ride along with me."

Mr. Webster looked relived. "Since Wayne is going anyhow, Ellie," he urged, "I'm sure Beatrice would trust *you* with the medicine. And she has written a letter to her daughter, apparently a very important letter, that she wants delivered personally."

"Of course, Paw. If Wayne is sure that I won't be a bother to him."

"It would more likely be the other way around,

ma'am." Wayne twisted his lips into a smile that did not include the rest of his face. He limped off in the direction of the feedlot where the horses were penned.

"I'll get ready quickly, Paw," Ellie said. "I wouldn't want to delay Wayne." She hurried inside to change to her best gingham dress. Her fingers coaxed her hair into a shapely coil, anchoring it with a pin. Almost without thinking, she secured the front of her dress with a brooch that had belonged to her mother.

The trip was pleasant enough, the day cool. With a bittersweet ache, Ellie relived history's bygone days as they neared Cripple Creek's low crossing where the shallow water tumbled over the pebbles, singing its liquid song.

Farther on, a big, lightning-abused cottonwood tree hung out over an elbow in the stream. This was where her family used to stop for a picnic when they went to town, breaking up the trip for the younger children. Even her mother would shed her shoes for a wade in the rivulet. "A body's feet never gets too old to enjoy this toe-tickling feeling," she said.

Much to Ellie's relief, Wayne didn't try to make small talk. As their buggy neared town, they meshed with a congestion of others that made a living stream of the hard-packed dirt road. "Everybody in the county must have decided to do their shopping today," Ellie commented. "Just look at the people!"

"A typical Saturday in town," Wayne nodded. "It's always like this."

The buggy slowed, and the road filled with potholes. Ellie gripped the side of the seat as the wheels fell in and out of the washes, thumping along.

Strange noises and smells pulled at her senses. Horses and riders pressed so close to each other that she feared someone would be crushed in the melee. Greetings and farewells made her feel sick and dizzy. Could she live—and work—in *this?* Her heart knew the answer. Mr. Samuelson's option was the lesser of the two evils.

On the square, vendors displayed their wares. Locally made food and handcrafts lined the boardwalks: harnesses, milking stools, woven baskets, sacks of tobacco, and bric-a-brac. Men were calling, laughing, and jesting. The whole of it was vulgar to Ellie's sensitive nature. Even the air was stale, contaminated.

"Where would you like to go, Miss Webster?" Wayne asked.

"Beatrice's daughter works at the soda fountain in the drugstore." Ellie had to raise her volume so that she might be heard above the din. "I'll need to go there."

From the town's center, a network of narrow, sordid streets crawled away to unknown wickedness. Wayne turned down one of these cobbled streets.

"My business shouldn't take very long," he said. "If you'll wait in the store, I will return for you when I'm finished."

Ellie was gripped with apprehension akin to desperation. She felt vulnerable, helpless. Nothing had prepared her for the world's changes while she sat on a farm nursing her dying dream, clinging to her wooden heart.

Wayne helped her from the wagon, lifting her to the boardwalk with capable arms. She was surprised at his strength, his physical power. He accompanied her to the door of the business place to make sure she reached her destination in safety. Then he was gone, swallowed in the swarm of milling people. She wanted to call him back, to beg him not to leave her. But that was childish, of course. He would think her foolish.

Finding Wancille posed no problem. With her rouged face, she might have been a younger version of her billowy mother. Only Wancille was more loose limbed and willow slim.

"Hello," Ellie said, feeling out of place. "I'm Ellie—"
"Ellie? Ellie who?"
"Webster."
"I don't believe I know you." Wancille tapped a red fingernail on the wooden counter and stared at Ellie as though she came from the shelf of a curio shop.
"Your mother calls me Eleanor."
"Oh, Eleanor! Of course. I've heard my mother speak of you and those heavenly berry pies. I'm dying to taste one of them. I'm pleased to meet you, I'm sure. If you had mentioned to me your *proper* name in the first—" Wancille stopped to roll her made-up eyes at an eager cowboy who slouched past the counter.
"Your mother sent this letter by me." Ellie only had half of Wancille's attention. "I came for medication. She's ill."

Wancille took the letter from Ellie and gave an unladylike snort. "Beatrice ill? Ha! Don't let her fool you, kiddo. She is as healthy as a mule and twice as balky. Beatrice turns 'ill' on and off at will. Better said, she's upset about something. I dare say she'll make that revelation in this letter." She disrespectfully tossed the letter onto the counter and slapped her hand on it. "But I'll read it, of course. I'm glad it's you who puts up with her whims and not me, kiddo. I put up with her for twenty-two years.

You can take a turn at it now." Another young man, a lean, stringy chap with a barbed-wire hair style and porkchop sideburns, slunk down the aisle, diverting Wancille's attention again. "Hi, Luther!" she gushed.

"Howdy, babe." His words rolled like marbles around the brown stump of a cheap cigar with a sickening, musky odor.

Ellie turned to leave, embarrassed by Wancille's familiarity with the men customers.

"Are you in such a rush?" Wancille asked. "I've just met you."

"Not . . . really."

"Then come on back by my counter when you're finished purchasing Beatrice's medicine, and I'll treat you to a soda. The proprietor doesn't mind. I just put it on my ticket, and he subtracts it from my paycheck. The fun of working here is sharing sodas. A *stepsister*. Imagine that! I can't believe Beatrice finally found a man that would put up with her!" She cackled.

The prospects of a complimentary soda did not interest Ellie so much as a place to sit out of the crowded mob. She hoped that Wayne would return for her soon. She was ready to leave this soul-disquieting place. The longer she stayed, the dirtier she felt. Never could she live and work here. Never!

She had just taken her first sip of the slushy-cold soda when Wayne slipped in and took the swivel stool beside her. "All done?" he asked.

"All done."

"Then I'll have a soda, too, to cool myself off, and we'll head back to the farm. I care little for city life."

"Nor I." Her voice was flat.

Between squeezing lemons for her sodas, Wancille talked with Ellie, ignoring Wayne. Ellie supposed Wayne was not the type Wancille cared to flirt with, and she was glad. "I took a peek at Beatrice's letter." She curled her ruby red lips. "She tells me that you are marrying Emil Samuelson. And *that's* why she is ill, of course. I knew there was a reason. Somehow she has learned that Mr. Samuelson has much more money than she thought. You see, I wanted to marry him myself at one time, and she forbade it. Now it seems she'd give an eyetooth if I would. With Beatrice, money talks. You'll find that she'll either have looks or money. Well, it serves Beatrice right. . . . Congratulations, Eleanor! That brooch you are wearing— is that a gift from Emil?"

Ellie's hand groped for the pin. "N-no. This belonged to my own precious mother. It was given to her by her mother."

Confused and sore-hearted, Ellie left most of her soda untouched and sought the solace of the buggy, the vehicle that would take her from this deplorable place and Wancille's wandering eyes.

As she neared the buggy, she caught sight of a fleeing man, retreating from behind her carriage. It looked like Jed Greaves. And in a blur, she saw the back of a shirt disappear down an alleyway. A shirt that she had mended and sewed buttons on: her brother Jimmy's shirt.

CHAPTER TWENTY-TWO

Framed!

The reins lay loose in Wayne's weather-chapped hands, and the horses chose their own pace.

"I didn't know that you planned to marry the schoolteacher."

Ellie tried to analyze Wayne's tone of voice. Did she detect disappointment? Or was it reproof—or regret?

What she meant to be a laugh came out a thin tremolo. "I didn't know it myself until yesterday. Mr. Samuelson came to supper to lay his plans before my father. It seems they have my future pretty well decided."

"You mean, it isn't *your* idea to marry the man?"

"Not at all."

"Then why would you agree to a marriage you did not choose?"

"Considering the alternative, it is the lesser of two evils."

"The alternative?"

"My father's wife says that one of us must go. Either she will go, or I must go myself."

"But you were there first."

"True. But to spare my father the disgrace of a broken marriage, I must leave my father's home."

"There's something wrong when the tail wags the dog . . . ."

"My father will pay a great price for peace. I'm afraid I'm a part of that price. I thought that I might be able to find employment in town and earn my own wage. But after these few hours spent there, I know that I could never adjust to city life. I'm a country girl."

"What does that have to do with a marriage to Mr. Samuelson? He's not exactly a farm boy."

"He has offered to provide a home for me anywhere I wish and share his wealth with me as an alternative to a job in town."

"Once you said that you had been in love and could never love again. Do you love this man?"

"Of course not."

"Then you are not being honest with him. . . ."

"I've been quite straightforward with Mr. Samuelson, sir. I have concealed none of my feelings. He knows that I do not love him. I told him so. Furthermore, he has told me quite as frankly that he does not love me. Love has nothing to do with the . . . the arrangement."

"But Miss Webster! How could you . . . I mean, I don't understand . . . a *loveless* marriage? A marriage without love would be no marriage at all. What a shameful farce!"

"I'm afraid that's what it amounts to."

"Without love there can be no . . . happiness."

"Sir, my happiness is laid away in a grave next to my lost love. Both are lying in the same cemetery alongside my dead dreams. I knew the beauty of love once. My heart belonged to a prince of a man named Daniel Brock. I know I shall never love anyone else. My hope of happiness . . . is gone. It perished with my Daniel.

"Of course, Mr. Samuelson disagrees with me that I ever was in love—that *anyone* has ever been in love. According to his philosophy, love is an imaginary state of being that is conceived in a mental myth and born to emotional fantasy. He would like the word taken from the human vocabulary, I'm sure."

"But *you* don't believe that tommyrot, do you, Miss Webster?"

"I'm . . . I'm trying to get things sorted out in my mind right now, sir. I'm . . . not sure what I do believe. I guess you could say survival is my priority just now. And I'm not sure that I wouldn't be better off if I didn't survive!"

"Do you believe there is a God, Miss Webster?" Now his voice had swung to deep conviction.

"Oh, yes!"

"I'm afraid one can't believe there is a God without believing in love. Because God *is* love. And God so loved us that He wrapped Himself in flesh to save us. Do you believe that?"

"Oh, by all means!"

"Then how could you enter an earthly relationship so sacred without love? The apostle Paul said a man ought to love his wife as Christ loved the church."

"Mr. Samuelson explained this as a marriage of convenience. I suppose it will be as if I am working for him—cooking, ironing, mending, cleaning—in exchange for his financial care of me. He will not be obligated to anything emotional, and neither will I. Could it be so much worse than working for a wage in a wicked city and caring for myself for the remainder of my time on this earth?"

"Pardon me, Miss Webster, but that is the most *selfish* approach I have ever heard any man take!" Wayne's already contorted face became even more misshapen.

"Selfish?"

"That's what I said. And that's what I meant to say. A man who will not give his heart to the woman he weds loves only himself. He doesn't need a wife; he needs a common servant. Let him hire one!" Wayne's voice was strong. "When is this . . . this mock ceremony to take place?"

"I don't know, sir. Right away, I suppose. Beatrice wants me out when school is dismissed for the summer."

"And the man openly admits he doesn't love you?"

"He loves nothing but teaching."

"Are you aware, Miss Webster, that what you are telling me is against the Bible, against God's divine will?"

"N-no." His reproach stung her. "At least, I hadn't thought of it in those terms."

"God's Word says a woman should reverence her husband. Can you respect Mr. Samuelson and hold him in esteem under the conditions you have just described to me?"

"I think it would be quite . . . impossible, sir."

"Then I should think—"

Wayne didn't finish his sentence. A racing horse pulled up beside the carriage, and the rider motioned Wayne to stop. Wayne pulled in on the reins.

"Is something wrong?" Ellie asked.

"There must be."

"I'm Officer Hardman." The huge man touched his wide-brimmed felt hat. "And they say I'm aptly named." He tapped the badge that was on their off side and ordered Wayne to alight. The silver on the man's spurs caught rays from the sun and threw them into Ellie's face, almost blinding her.

"It has been reported that you are concealing intoxicating spirits in your vehicle." Ellie's curious eyes found the two pistols the man wore in his holsters. They didn't look friendly.

"You must be mistaken." Wayne did not flinch.

"May I have a look?"

"Certainly." Wayne lifted Ellie from the buggy, and the officer began an inch-by-inch search. Presently he pulled a jug of whiskey from beneath the seat. "Ah, here it is. This is illegal, you understand."

"Sir, I have no idea how it got there."

"That's the usual story, mister."

"I'm sorry, I—"

"There's a stiff fine for the offense. And for those who cannot pay the fine, it's a trip to jail."

"If I may take the lady home first, please?"

"The lady will have to get home the best way she can, I'm afraid. I have no assurance that you would bother to return. Law is law. When one breaks the law, one can expect to suffer the penalty for breaking that law."

Ellie's mind reached back, trying to find pieces to the puzzle. The man she saw slipping away from the buggy when she came out of the drugstore . . .

One thing she knew: she couldn't let Mr. Hardman take Wayne to jail. He was innocent!

"Sir!" she said. "This man didn't put the bottle there."

I'm . . . pretty sure I know who did it!"

"Until we have proof otherwise, I'm afraid we have to assume that he did, miss. He has been found with the incriminating evidence."

"How . . . how much is the fine?"

"Twenty-five dollars, ma'am."

Ellie unlatched her brooch with fumbling fingers. "Here, sir." She handed it to Officer Hardman. "This heirlom belonged to my grandmother. It's from the Old World, and it is worth more than twice the fine. Please safeguard it until we can prove our innocence."

"Don't, Miss Webster!" objected Wayne. "I don't mind going to prison. Really, I don't!"

But Ellie was persistent. "I'll get my pin back," she said. "And furthermore, I don't want to walk home."

Mr. Hardman's monstrous horse seemingly spun around in midair at his command, and the officer was off in a whirlwind of dust kicked up by the thundering hooves. In his pocket was the valuable brooch.

Why had Jed Greaves planted the bottle in the buggy? And who knew about it to make the report to the constable? Was this Jed's way of intimidating her and frightening her away from town? Or was the deed an act of jealous rage? Nothing made sense.

CHAPTER TWENTY-THREE
The Two-Timer

*T*ravis was having problems of his own. Ellie had sensed it for some time, but when he took his fishing pole and went to the creek instead of going to school, her awareness grew to real concern.

After she put away the breakfast jelly, dipped the sour milk into crocks to clabber, and shooed the last stray fly out the screen door with her apron, she made her way to the stream where she knew she would find her brother.

He wasn't fishing. A pole lay on the bank undisturbed as he sat staring across the stream into the mutiny of tangled limbs and moss-robed rocks. His chin rested in his cupped hands. He remained motionless and showed no surprise when he saw Ellie picking her way down the bank.

She dropped to the grassy shore beside him and folded her legs up under her skirt, circling them with her arms. Still he made no effort to move.

"What's wrong, Travis? Something has been bothering you for days."

"Yes, Ellie, but I'll not dump my problems on you. You have a heart full of cares of your own with Beatrice. I should be man enough to handle my own troubles."

"You've grown up so much, Travis. Just since Wayne came. Wayne has been good for you."

"Yes, he has. He's taught me so much. Mainly, he's taught me to conquer myself. There's real triumph in self-discipline, he says. But I have so far to go yet, an' I'll be obliged to go on without Wayne. You know Paw is lettin' him go, don't you?"

"Yes, I overheard."

"It's because of *her*, ain't it, Ellie?"

"I'm afraid it is."

"She messes ever'thing up! I 'spected she was behind this, too. She's always hated Wayne. But he just goes right on bein' nice to her anyhow. Wayne offered to stay on without any pay at all, you know, if Paw needed him."

"No, I didn't know."

"But Paw said, no, it would be best if he moved on. That's when I figgered it was her idea to send Wayne apacking."

"When will he be leaving, Travis?"

"In about a week, I think. He wants to help Paw harvest th' grain. He's tryin' to get something out of pawn. When he first come, Paw promised him a horse. He's goin' to sell the horse to get whatever this is. I thought he said a *brooch*, but that didn't make sense. I'm sure I misunderstood him. Sometimes he doesn't talk very plain because of his scars."

The brooch. Wayne wanted to get her mother's brooch back to her before he left.

"I know you'll make a man of yourself whether

Wayne is here or not, Travis. You've got a good head start on it this last six months. I'm proud of you."

"After all those prayers with Wayne, well, I've been changed around inside, and I really want to make something of my life. I've been workin' hard at school, Ellie. I really have. Wayne helped me every evenin' with my homework, and I'll make all my grades. Wayne has a good education. He can figure in his head faster than most people can figure on paper.

"Since he came, I decided I wanted to go on to the academy. I just lack a year of high school. But now— now—" His voice broke.

"Now what, Travis? You can still go to the academy. I . . . I think I'll be in a position to help you financially by then."

"Paw says that, with Wayne gone, I'll have to help on the farm next year. Paw can't take care of the croppin' all by himself. So why bother to go back to school if I've got to quit anyhow?"

"Don't give up yet, Travis. I . . . I'm working on a plan that might help us all."

"You're not going to try to go to work for a wage, are you, Ellie?"

"N-no. Just help me pray that I'll know what to do about an offer that's been made me. Is that all that's on your mind?"

"No. There's a million other things. I'm still worried about Jimmy hangin' out with Jed Greaves."

"That bears some praying, too."

"Did Mr. Samuelson come to our house for supper that day to talk about Jimmy?"

"No. He came for a visit and to—"

"I don't understand why he is lettin' Jimmy get by with so much lately. It's like he's blind to Jimmy's absences and his poor conduct. Purposely blind. Mr. Samuelson's mind hasn't been on teachin' for several days now. And that's not at all like Mr. Samuelson: he eats, breathes, and sleeps teaching!"

"You are a very perceptive young man, Travis."

"If you want to know what *I* think, I think he's got his mind on a *woman.*"

Ellie turned her head away and picked at a stem of weed. "I'm afraid so. He's making plans to marry."

"I thought so! I caught him flirting last Saturday."

"Last Saturday? Flirting?"

"Yep. Remember when me an' Paw went into town for more bitters for Beatrice? While Paw got th' bitters, I went to th' soda fountain for an ice. An' who should be there titterin' with the lady behind th' counter but the schoolteacher himself!"

"You mean Mr. Samuelson was flirting with *Wancille?*"

"I don't know th' lady's name. But she had the reddest lips and nails of anyone I've ever seen! I wouldn't be surprised if her *toenails* wasn't painted, too! That Jezebel and her catch were laughing an' carrying on something scandalous!"

"Did . . . did Mr. Samuelson see you?"

"Not for awhile. His attention was bottled up in that gaudy woman. But when I said, 'Hello, Mr. Samuelson,' he recognized me."

"What did he do then?"

"He turned all kinds of red. I figured he didn't want one of his pupils to catch him courtin'. As if it was any of my business what he does on his hours off! He stammered an' stuttered an' said he hoped I would forget th' little funnin' he was having with an old friend of his. I told him I didn't find it any problem—that I expected I'd enjoy th' company of a girl myself some day."

Ellie smiled. "Beatrice will be glad to hear of fate's latest twist to the drama."

"What difference would it make to Beatrice about the teacher or the soda-fountain girl?"

"Wancille is Beatrice's daughter. She wants the young lady to marry Mr. Samuelson for his money." She gave a surface-only laugh.

"Do you find it funny?"

"Indeed I do! As I started to tell you, Mr. Samuelson came here to supper to ask Paw for *my* hand in marriage."

"Don't spoof me, Ellie."

"I'm not spoofing. I'm as serious as our mother's grave."

"You weren't going to marry *Mr. Samuelson,* were you, Ellie?"

"Well, to be truthful, Travis, I was giving it some consideration—that is, before today—before you told me what you just did."

"But, Ellie, I had no idea you loved Mr. Samuelson."

"I didn't."

"Oh, Ellie. Now you do have me confused. You would marry someone without lovin' him?"

"Mr. Samuelson said it has been done. It would be like working for him, really. He would provide me a home, and he even offered to help with your education."

"I couldn't have accepted it, Ellie. Not like that. Maybe Mr. Samuelson said people marry without love, but it's not done by . . . by Christians. By heathens, maybe."

"I came to see if I could help with your problems. Now I find that I have a problem of my own. A brand-new problem."

"What is it, Ellie?"

"Since I won't be marrying the two-timing Mr. Samuelson, and Wancille will, I don't know what I'll do."

Travis grinned. "I think that's God's problem, and I'd say that bears some prayin', Ellie. Remember, Wayne says God has a pattern for our lives, and He hasn't lost the pattern!"

"You're not going to school today?"

"Yes, I'm runnin' late, but I'd better get myself a move on, I guess. Would you mind takin' my pole back to the house an' puttin' it up for me?"

"Give your teacher a message for me, Travis." Ellie jumped up and brushed the grass from her skirt. "Tell him I won't be in for my lesson this afternoon."

CHAPTER TWENTY-FOUR

The Accident

Spring stepped aside for a day of presummer heat. Ellie took off her slat bonnet and fanned her sweaty face with its stiff brim. She would need to bring up some ice from the icehouse. Her father hated warm tea after a day of hot field work.

"Wayne's leavin' tomorrow, Ellie," Travis told her. "I found some first-ripe blackberries, an' I thought you could make us a pie as a goin' away surprise for him. He especially likes your berry pies." Travis set the bucket of berries on the cupboard. "Paw says it's ridiculous to keep a hired hand when he has strappin' sons who can do the work without pay. Wayne said he would be glad to be counted a son, but Paw ain't in no adoptin' mood."

For the whole of the day, the water bucket had not been refilled, nor did Wayne show up for work. What if he had gone on ahead of schedule to avoid the goodbyes? The thought brought Ellie a vague inner distress that she could not account for. They had all depended on him—and his prayers—more than she realized. He was like a rock or a stalwart tree: something you saw every day but failed to appreciate its value, its shade, until one day you recognized that you needed the strength that only it could provide.

Jimmy came on the run, his hair disheveled and his eyes wild. "Quick, Ellie, where's Paw?" Had her brother been drinking?

"I don't know, Jimmy." She threw him a cautious glance, trying to decide whether or not he was sober. "Why do you need Paw?"

"Ellie! If we can't find Paw, *you've* got to help me."

"Slow down, and tell me why you are so excited, Jimmy. Have you been drinking?"

"No, Ellie!" He started to cry. *"Please* help me!"

"Has one of the boys been hurt?"

"Oh, yes—I mean—oh, Ellie! Wayne has been accidentally shut up in the icehouse for a long time. I found him there, and I think . . . he's *dead.*" Jimmy's fear-ridden eyes pleaded with her to help, to say that Wayne wasn't dead. "We missed him, but we just supposed that he . . . left without sayin' goodbye. All us boys knew he was dreadin' the leavin'."

Ellie found herself stumbling along with Jimmy toward the small building where Wayne lay. "Oh, God, let him be alive," she prayed aloud, not even hearing the urgent entreaty of her own words.

From another direction, Mr. Webster raced toward them, panting, with Travis a step behind. "What's happened?"

"Jimmy found Wayne in the icehouse. He may be dead." A wave of weakness washed over Ellie, its undertow almost taking her to the ground. "And I guess it was

... I ... who locked him in," she groaned. "I saw the door ajar and bolted it from the outside, not knowing anyone was ... in there." Characteristic of the gentleman that Wayne was, he had been trying to help her by bringing up ice from the pit of sawdust on this sultry day. And this was his reward!

A big man unconscious is a piteous sight, and Ellie turned her head away when they lifted him from the floor of wood shavings. Was he alive?

"Go for a quilt, Ellie," commanded her father, and she was only too willing to flee the scene.

When she returned, Mr. Webster was massaging Wayne's chest while Travis and Jimmy rubbed his hands and arms. "The quilt, Ellie!" shouted her father. "We want to bring his body back to its normal temperature."

"Is he ... alive?" The words crippled out, crutched up by fervent hope.

"Barely."

What if he should die, the fault being her own? He had no family, no one to mourn his going. He had once said that no one would grieve for his departure from this life. He would probably be glad to join his young wife and baby in God's painless, tearless paradise.

Chances were, no one would remember a trustworthy, unworldly farmhand who asked little of life save a sense of peace and harmony with himself and his fellow man. Undistinguished and commonplace, his short life would be forgotten like an unknown soldier who perished on the battlefield, laid in an unmarked grave.

But some things Ellie could never forget. The garden that even now produced fresh radishes, onions, lettuce, early sweet peas ... How apologetic he had been when he came dangerously close to chopping down the wrong tree for firewood, her special tree with its wooden heart . . . The time he showed up at the Greaveses as her "wings" of rescue from the lustful Jed . . . His interest in Jimmy's welfare . . . The changes he had wrought in Travis's life . . . The day he eased little Dee's swollen gums with the ice and nearly gave himself away as once being a father . . . He didn't finish his title, but she knew that "Daddy" had almost slipped out. Then there had been the trip to Springdale when he tried, with his spiritual insight, to discourage the idea of her marrying Mr. Samuelson. He had been right, of course. What he said had a biblical foundation. She would file these tokens away along with her memories of Daniel.

What had she done to repay this unassuming stranger for the many thoughtful deeds he had done? With a pang of remorse, she realized that she had never done a thing. He had given unreservedly, asking nothing in return. Now he would probably not even live to taste his "going away" blackberry pie. Was it fair?

Ellie's thoughts resurrected the prayers she had heard him pray in the middle of the dark, snowy nights above her room. Interceding heart-prayers they were.

"We'll take him to the house, boys," Mr. Webster was saying. "If he is to come out of this, he will need around-the-clock care. And there's no one to give it but us."

"You can put him in our room, Paw," Jimmy spoke up in a reedy man's voice. "We've got th' south window. It'll be coolest there in th' hot of th' day." Travis nodded his assent.

Beatrice filled the back door with her imposing bulk. "What on earth, Ronald . . . ?"

"Please move aside, Beatrice." Mr. Webster's words were short, direct. "We have a very ill man here."

"If he's hurt, take him into town for his cure, Ronald. He's just a hired hand. By all means, don't try to nurse him *here!* We don't have room for ailing drifters in this house."

Mr. Webster ignored her. "Let's make him comfortable, boys. Lay him down, and take off his boots."

"Where are you taking him?" Beatrice trailed along, unsympathetic and demanding. "No, not to *that* room, Ronald. With the hot weather coming on, I had planned to have that room for myself. I need that cool south breeze for my headaches. Put him in the attic, or take him back to the barn, please."

If Mr. Webster heard her, he gave no indication of it. "That's right, boys. Don't take the quilt off yet. Let him warm up completely." They moved to their destination with Beatrice sputtering objections.

"Ellie, I'm afraid a great deal of Wayne's recovery will depend on you." Mr. Webster appealed to his daughter.

"Impossible, Ronald!" cut in Beatrice with dogged persistence. "I have a *ghastly* headache, and Eleanor should be starting to prepare supper right now. I'm much too ill to cook tonight. And I'm *famished.* I think I shall faint if supper is delayed. And, may I say, if you expect *me* to help care for a homeless waif, you've rattled the wrong door latch."

"Oh, no, Beatrice. It never entered my mind that you would turn a hand to help." His words took no detours. And they bit deep and hard. "But this is *my* house, and I will offer an injured man a place to die. I'm sure he would do the same for me."

"Sometimes, Ronald," she said with a pretense of patient resignation, "I think you haven't the intelligence you were born with."

"Be grateful, Beatrice." He said it evenly. "Because if I had, you probably would never have talked me into marrying you."

Beatrice left the room with clipped, offended steps.

Ellie moved in close to her father. She looked down at the form on the bed and grew pensive. Would Daniel really mind so much if she gave just a bit of her devotion to a man in desperate need? A man who loved their God, too? Just until he was strong again? Did she not owe it to the stranger since she had occasioned his hurt?

He had lent her aid, saving her from the passions of a man with soiled motives. And now must she not be a grateful debtor? Daniel would expect nothing less of her.

If she did not nurture the man, he would die. But then he would probably die anyway.

CHAPTER TWENTY-FIVE

Back to the Well

---

*B*eatrice, no longer the center of attention, grew petulant as the week wore on. Her agitation congealed into vexation.

"Why don't you move the sick man to Doc Hawley's office, Ronald?" she plagued. "Surely he has a room the man can occupy until the mortician is called upon to embalm the body. Shakespeare said, 'To everything there's a season.' Your hired man has had his season here and he's none the better, so it's time you move him somewhere else."

"Wayne is in no condition to be moved, Beatrice. The doctor said so."

When she saw that her nagging was getting her nowhere, Beatrice tried a different approach. "I never could abide sick rooms, Ronald, even when I was a child. I must ask you to consider my delicate nature in this matter. Either you will have the man removed, or I shall absent myself for an indefinite time. My nerves simply will not abide this . . . this *depressed* atmosphere. Why, I can hardly breathe—"

"Where would you like to go, Beatrice?" Mr. Webster asked, and the abashed look on Beatrice's face would have made a story plot.

"You mean, you won't try to detain me, Ronald?"

"No, Beatrice. Go where you will."

"I . . . I think I shall go spend some time with my daughter, Wancille. I will return when this man is dead and gone."

"Jimmy, you're nigh on to being a man now. You'll turn sixteen next week. I'm sure I can trust you to take Beatrice to town in the buggy."

Beatrice stuffed her personal belongings into her portmanteau and slammed the lid shut with an attention-seeking bang. Jimmy picked the travel case up for her and strode out the door, his shoulders square.

Ellie cast an uneasy glance after Jimmy. Could he be trusted to behave himself with the buggy in a town that provided so many temptations? What if he met up with Jed—and the bottle? She should have told her father about the trouble Jimmy had been sliding into. But he had been so preoccupied since he married Beatrice. If only her father had sent Travis instead!

After Jimmy left with the complaining Beatrice, Ellie turned her unfocused vision out the screened window where a distant cluster of jadegreen trees hid a small pasture. She was tired. Her succession of day duties and night vigils bumped together, making her feet uncoordinated and her hands clumsy. But she refused to slacken her self-imposed pace.

Almost shyly, Travis approached her. His eyes were bloodshot; he had been crying. "I've been out to th' barn to Wayne's altar, Ellie. I've been prayin' for him. I don't believe he's goin' to die. Really, I don't. With your good care an' my prayers, we'll see him through. He's a real man. And the world is shortchanged on real men. I don't see how we can afford to lose any more.

"I've been doing some thinkin'. I want to take over where Wayne left off. When Wayne does get well, he'll be movin' on to help someone else. Could . . . could you show me how to milk th' cows, Ellie? I tried this mornin', but I can't seem to get the push an' pull of it."

His solicitousness touched Ellie. She had noticed the eggs already sitting on the side cupboard just where Wayne always put them. Travis had also brought up a block of ice, wrapped in burlap, for Mr. Webster's tea.

"Wayne will be proud of you. And, yes, we'll go to the cow lot after a while, and I'll teach you to milk."

Mr. Webster came to check on Wayne. "Has there been any change, Ellie?" He laid his hand on her sagging shoulder.

"None, Paw. He does swallow broth, though. As long as I can get nourishment down him, I think we have a chance."

"That's what the doctor said. The doctor thinks he may have suffered a severe head injury when he passed out and fell. I . . . hope we aren't fighting a losing battle."

"We'll fight, Paw: win, lose, or draw. We Websters are fighters, remember." She tried on a smile that fit poorly. "We come by it honestly."

"I need to talk to you, Ellie, if you can come into the sitting room for a minute."

"Sure, Paw." Ellie followed him; she dropped wearily into the stuffed chair with its antimacassar-covered back and arms.

"I'm in some trouble I've never had to face before. Beatrice has been buying things on credit, and I didn't know about it. She has charged goods at the grocery store, the millinery, and through mail-order books. When I found it out, I put a freeze on the accounts. She won't be happy about it, but I . . . had to do it. I've never been a slave to a bad debt in my life until now. By selling off some of the cattle, I can pull out. Beatrice's irresponsible actions have affected all of you, and . . . I'm sorry."

"Oh, Paw, why did you . . ." Ellie stopped, embarrassed at the question that threatened to surface.

Mr. Webster finished her question. "Why did I marry Beatrice? Well, there's no fool like an old fool, they say, Ellie. Seems men are more apt to do foolish things on an impulse than women. The pride in me fell to the flattery of Beatrice. I've been terribly lonely since your mother left me. And I thought that you, stuck out here with all us menfolk, needed some woman company. Beatrice set herself up as a ready-made answer to all these things.

"Now, a vow is a vow, and I vowed to cling to her until death. But she's making it hard. There'll have to be some changes if she is to stay on here with me and my children."

"I understand, Paw. It's been hard for us all. Wayne said it wasn't right for the *tail* to wag the *dog*." Ellie wondered whether Mr. Webster's surprised look was because she mentioned Wayne or because of the truth of the statement itself.

"I've never heard it put just that way, but I couldn't better it." He chuckled. "I wish I had set my foot down right from the start. It'll be harder now, like chopping down a weed after you've let it grow tall and tough. And I may lose Beatrice. That in itself wouldn't be world's end, except that I'll be losing you, too, when you marry. And how will I ever manage to feed and care for four boys by myself?"

"When I marry? What do you mean, Paw?"

"Why, you'll be marrying soon!"

Ellie had quite forgotten that she was supposed to marry Emil Samuelson. "I have no plans of marrying—*ever!*"

"But what about Mr. Samuelson? He said—"

"Fortunately, I never agreed to marry Mr. Samuelson. The arrangement was his idea, not mine. Did he, did *anyone* ask my opinion or hear me say that I would agree to the proposal he made?"

Mr. Webster screwed his face into a perplexed study. "Why, now that I think of it, I don't believe you said a word. . . ."

"I didn't. Wayne said that a marriage on Mr. Samuelson's terms could not be God's will." She hadn't planned to bring Wayne into the conversation again. "You see, Mr. Samuelson never loved me. He frankly admitted that he did not love me."

"Then why . . . ?"

"It was to be an arrangement for convenience. I would cook and clean, and my reward would be the privilege of sharing his home and his name."

"And you told him you couldn't marry him on those terms?"

"No. He's changed his mind. And I've done a lot of speculating about that, too. Beatrice's daughter figures in this somewhere. When Beatrice returns from her visit, if she returns, I think she'll be announcing the engagement of Wancille. To Mr. Samuelson."

"You're not saying the teacher proposed to you to provoke Beatrice's daughter to jealousy?"

"It's probably even more complicated than that. I think they have had a long-standing courtship that Beatrice bitterly opposed. But when Beatrice found out just how much money Mr. Samuelson actually had and that she might lose his bank account to *me*, she was quite eager to have him for her son-in-law. Don't you remember what she said that night Mr. Samuelson came for supper? She said she would indeed love to have him for *her* son-in-law. She didn't mean her *step*son-in-law. Unless I miss my guess, she and Wancille are plotting and planning the girl's wedding to Mr. Samuelson right now. My mail-order catalog is missing."

"I'm glad to know you are not leaving, my daughter."

Ellie took the near-empty water bucket and started for the well. A heavy fretwork of grapevines hung from the trees. This was her favorite time of the year, the time of the year when Daniel had given her the heart on the tree . . . her wooden heart.

Travis came on the run and reached for the wire handle. "Here, Ellie, let me get the water for you."

"Thank you, Travis." She smiled up at him, noticing for the first time how much taller he was than she. "After today, you can keep the water bucket filled. But just this once, I *want* to go to the well myself."

CHAPTER TWENTY-SIX

The Anniversary

When the knock came at the front door, Ellie jumped. She had been watching for Jimmy all afternoon, concerned that he had not returned promptly from taking Beatrice into town.

But it was Mazie who stood at the door with her silly, girlish grin. A frazzled braid, tied at the end with twine, hung down her back. She balanced her baby, clad only in a dingy diaper, on her left hip. Milk from a recent feeding trickled down the child's chin and into the creases of her fat neck.

Ellie held up her hand. "I can't keep the baby today. Please accept my apologies. I'd love to, but I've supper to cook for the whole family and broth to fix for our hired man."

"I didn't come to get you to keep th' baby this time, Ellie. I came to talk about . . . other things."

"You heard about the accident, didn't you?"

"Accident? What accident? Did one of your'n get hurt?"

"Wayne, the farmhand, was closed up in the icehouse for several hours and couldn't get out. It's very near airtight in that little place, and he passed out. He hasn't regained consciousness. I thought one of the boys would have told Jed."

"Jed ain't been home for several days. Up to his devilment in town, I'm sure. It's a habit of his'n to go in when he gets bored—which is pretty often lately. He ain't never stayed away this long, but I never fret over him. Me and Greaves get along better when he's not there. I wouldn't mind if'n he'd stay away more. But how did your hired hand get shut up in the icehouse?"

"I—I did it myself. I didn't know he was there, and I bolted the door."

"You takin' care of him here?"

"Yes. Paw says he's too sick to move. We've had the doctor out several times, but he says he can't do any more for him than what we are doing. He said he likely suffered a concussion."

"A cussin'?"

"An injury inside his head. It's as if he is asleep and can't wake up."

"Would it be okay if I come in an' see him?"

"I suppose so."

Ellie led the way to the south bedroom where Wayne lay quiet and white. Mazie sat her baby on the floor. "Can I do anything to help?" she asked. "I'd be glad to."

"I'm afraid there's no one but God who can do anything. It's just a matter of time, the doctor says. He might wake up—and he might not."

The infant pulled herself up and took a tottering step to the bed where Wayne lay motionless. She placed her cherubic face against Wayne's arm and patted him. "Da-Da-Da!" she blubbered.

Mazie gave a comical little laugh. "Listen to her call him daddy! She thinks every man she sees is her daddy! She's learning to walk and to talk real fast now, Ellie."

Wayne's eyelids fluttered feebly, and he tried to open them. "He's—he's trying to wake up!" Ellie pulled the baby back. His lips twitched; then he went back into his comatose state.

Ellie's mind spun back to the scene in the barn where Wayne almost made his verbal disclosure. Was there some connection between this aimless wanderer and Mazie—or the baby? A deep mystery, almost tangible, tried to solve itself, the threads begging to be untangled. Why did Mazie want to see Wayne?

"Did you know Wayne before he came here, Mazie?"

"Oh, no, ma'am. I've never laid eyes on him."

"You seem to have such an interest. . . ."

"It's just that your farmhand has been so kind to us, plantin' us a big garden an' all. He didn't have to do that nor to repair th' house or stack firewood. Why, he has enough firewood stacked now to last us *two* winters! Now that he's all down n' out, I wish I could do somethin' for pay back."

Still Ellie groped for puzzle pieces. "The baby . . . is she yours, Mazie? Your very own, I mean."

"Why, of course. Mine and Greaves's. Who else's would she be?"

"What I meant was," Ellie stumbled on, "you didn't adopt her, did you?"

"Adopt her?"

"Take on somebody else's baby to raise?"

"Oh, lawsy, no! I *born* her. I hollered and carried on so when she was bein' born that Greaves up an' left th' place. Greaves's granny weighed 'er in on th' cotton scales. She weighed a good, healthy eight pound an' measured more'n half th' yardstick. Her name's really Delores, after Greaves's granny. That was her reward for stayin' with me when Greaves snuck out on me. I said right then an' there I hoped I never had to go through *that* again. An' I still mean it, but I'm kinda afraid there's another'n on th' way. An', lawsy, I *hope* not! But why do you ask if I borned her?"

"I just wondered."

"Lawsy, do you actually think I'd take somebody else's kid? Who'd want to be bothered with a youngun if they didn't have to?"

"Oh, I think it would be quite a noble thing to do, especially if the child's parents had met with tragedy."

"Not me. I say don't ask for extry mouths to feed and rags to warsh! Me an' Greaves had a big argument just this mornin' over his niece. She's wantin' to come an' spend th' whole summer with us. She's from Missoury, and, lawsy, is she an untamed thing! She's sowed enough wild oats that if half of them sprouted, it'd keep us in oatmeal the rest of our days. She swings when she walks and sets all the boys' hearts to doin' handsprings. A real looker—an' she knows it. She's sweet sixteen. You better watch your Jimmy if she comes. He'd just fall kersplat for her! I told Greaves he was askin' for dynamite to bring her here with a boy as unmanageable as Jeddy is. Get them two together, and, lawsy! One rowdy is enough, without bringin' in another to make *double* trouble. Ain't that what you think?"

"By all means." Wayne's face still twitched.

"Let's go back into the parlor, Mazie. We try to keep Wayne's room as quiet as possible."

"Seems it wouldn't make no matter if he can't hear nuthin' nohow." Mazie scooped up her child and deposited her in the sitting-room floor. "What I came for is to ask a question," she said. "We're having some trouble with th' land deal. We've got all th' papers signed, an' I won't have to go to town no more. But it's something 'bout th' keepin' of th' records at th' courthouse. They can't find out what's owed agin' it in taxes. Greaves wanted me to come over an' see if'n you folks would know 'bout when th' last folks that lived there left. Th' courthouse people need some kind of date to look for. Greaves said bein' as you was next-over neighbors, you just might recollect when they deserted th' place. At least th' year. If we can find out how long they been gone, he said, they could surely figger up th' taxes we owe by the amount of months or years they hadn't paid on it, see?"

Ellie had been to the well not more than two hours before. She had gone over every detail of the parting. Only this time, she had handled her broken dreams voluntarily and with a certain peace.

Now she smiled. "Yes, I remember the date quite well, Mrs. Greaves. It has been exactly six years. Six years ago today, Daniel Brock, who was my fiance, carved a heart on a tree with our initials inside. It was the last time I ever saw him. He left with his family six years ago tomorrow. The heart on the tree is still there. I went by to see it today."

"You was in love once?" Her voice held a little girlish thrill.

"Yes. Very much in love."

"Oooooooo!"

"But he's . . . dead now."

"Why, I—I wondered why you never got married, Ellie!"

"Now you know."

"An' you never could love nobody else?"

"I don't . . . think so."

"But how can you be . . . happy?"

"I've still got a wooden heart on a tree. And a dream. A very *beautiful* dream."

"I guess you're better off than me, Ellie. I hope your pretty dream never ends. Mine's turnin' to a nightmare since Greaves has started to drink so bad." Mazie hefted herself to her feet with a long sigh, pulled her sooty baby from behind the potbellied stove, and plodded toward the door.

Peace. Ellie felt one fleeting moment of real peace.

CHAPTER TWENTY-SEVEN
A Changed Boy

Supper came and went. A wedge of crackling bread, Jimmy's favorite, lay untouched.

The gong of the grandfather clock hammered out the hour, its metered twang falling silent after discharging its seven o'clock duty. The reverberation of the striking timepiece brought a terrible foreboding. Jimmy had not returned from Springdale.

"I hope Jimmy is all right," Ellie ventured, her fingers toying with a strand of honey-colored hair. "He should have been home before now."

"Jimmy is cottonin' to Beatrice," Mr. Webster said. "I know how she is when she gets in town. It's 'take me here' and 'take me there.' She gives no thought of time. When she turns Jimmy loose, he'll be on in. Don't fret yourself about him."

But Ellie did fret. What her father didn't know was that Jed Greaves was in town, too, and that could spell mischief. Ellie dug her way through a landslide of possibilities that tumbled over her mind. Drinking . . . gambling . . . girls . . .

The house closed in about her, giving her a suffocated feeling. She made her way to the porch. The sun kindled a fiery glow in the west and then left it as a careless traveler might abandon a campfire. Twilight began its patient work of extinguishing the last of the day's light, leaving the evening's colorful backdrop a flannel gray. Ellie shivered though the night was sultry.

The moon began its nightly watch. Mr. Webster stepped out onto the porch. "I just imagine Beatrice decided for Jimmy to stay on till morning so's he could take her some place else tomorrow," he said. "Jimmy knew we wouldn't be needin' th' buggy to make any trips. He's feeling the trust I put in him to see that Beatrice got where she wanted to go. I'm going to turn in for the night."

"I'll wait here a while longer, Paw. It's a pleasant enough night to be out."

A star appeared against the background of heathery sky. Then another. A falling meteor tailed a white path across the heavens like a white chalk mark across a blackboard, quickly erased. An old myth said someone died every time a star fell. *Please, God, don't let it be Wayne....*

One by one, her father and her brothers blew out their kerosene lamps and went to bed. But Ellie was in no mood for sleep. She and the wooden heart on the tree were celebrating their anniversary.

Minutes crawled by, turning to individual eternities. *Where is Jimmy?* The later it became, the more apprehension leeched onto Ellie's mind. Fear tore through her like a hurricane, battering her soul. Knowing Jimmy as she did, he would not "cotton" to Beatrice for this length of time. He would lose patience.

Ellie dozed, and her head doddered. A distant noise in the still of the night brought it up with a jerk. The fast clip of horses' hooves and the rattle of wheels heralded the approach of her father's buggy.

When Jimmy had unharnessed the horses, he came to sit by Ellie.

"You're late," she said.

"I've got a lot to tell you. It's been quite a day."

She waited, letting him set his own pace, disclose what he would, and withhold what he wished. But in her heart she prayed as she had been doing through the long hours.

"Jed's in jail."

"In jail?"

"Yes, and if it hadn't been for Wayne, I'd be right there with Jed."

"How could Wayne help you? He's in no shape to help anyone."

"Wayne has been workin' on me, on my attitude, since he set foot on this place last fall. But I've been rebellious. Jed was tough—and cocky. He dared me to do lots of things. Things I knew you and Paw wouldn't want me doin'. He called me a coward and a sissy if I didn't play his games.

"I did go along with him for a while. But all the time, I was running scared. A couple of times we almost got caught. I didn't do any of the stealin' or gamblin', but I helped Jed in the things he was doin'. Th' way I helped was by keeping a lookout, distractin' folks while he did the dirty work. He gave me a little money along. I felt grown-up, havin' money of my own.

"But when Wayne got hurt, I did some soulsearchin'. It hit me hard when I found him and thought he was dead.

The strangest thing happened. I looked at him, and he was still and quiet, but everything he had said about bein' honest, being' a man, kept screamin' out at me. It was as if Wayne was still talkin'; his mouth wasn't movin', but I could hear his voice inside me somewhere. He said I'd have to live in the 'house' I built for myself. I knew I'd never build a good life pairin' up with Jed Greaves. He'd tear down the good I could do faster than I could get it done. Wayne's accident—" Jimmy paused. "Do you believe there are any accidents, Ellie?"

"I'm beginning to doubt it."

"What happened to Wayne gave me a reason not to go into town with Jed this week. I didn't even bother to tell Jed about Wayne's accident. He didn't hold any likin' for Wayne. It made him mad to even hear Wayne's name mentioned.

"Well, without me along, it's no tellin' what all Jed got himself into. I think a lot of times I kept him from goin' too far. Jed drank a lot."

"You don't know why he's in jail?"

"Yes. There'd been some thievin' from the general store, and Mr. Hardman was on the watch for th' criminal. I didn't know Jed was still in town when I took Beatrice to the drugstore where her daughter works. I parked our buggy along front. Beatrice invited me to come on in and let her daughter do me a special lemon squeeze.

"Jed saw Paw's buggy out front, and I'm sure he thought it was you and Wayne come to town together again. You know, he's fiercely jealous of you and Wayne—"

"Jealous of me and Wayne? Whatever for, Jimmy?"

"He's always had it in his noggin that Wayne has eyes

for you. Him and Wayne has had some words concernin' you. And when Jed saw you and Wayne together in town that Saturday you went for the bitters, he just went nuts. I hate to admit it, but I was with him that day. He set me up as a watchdog while he planted that jug of whiskey under the seat of Paw's buggy. Then he went and squealed to the officer that he'd seen Wayne sneak it there. I know now that he was tryin' to get Wayne arrested and thrown in the hoosegow. That would get Wayne out of the way. He was good and mad when Mr. Hardman let Wayne go."

"But why didn't you tell the lawman?"

"I thought it was just a practical joke, and you can be sure that I wouldn't have let Wayne get sent up. I'd have snitched on Jed if it had come down to it. Jed let on to me that it was all in fun.

"Well, when Jed saw our rig in town today, he thought he'd do the same thing again. He had no watchdog this time, and Mr. Hardman did. The officer caught him red-handed, puttin' the bottle under th' seat like he did th' first time.

"When they arrested him an' searched him, they found th' exact amount of money that was missin' from the general store's cash box in Jed's pocket. So Mr. Hardman put two and two together and figured Jed was the one who stole the money and the one who hid the first bottle in the buggy.

"Mr. Hardman was waitin' for me when I came out of th' drugstore; he had Jed cuffed. When Jed saw it was me an' not Wayne, he begged me to keep th' officer from lockin' him up. His breath told me he'd passed th' time at a taproom somewhere. I told him I wouldn't lie for nobody. If he stole th' money, he'd have to take his rap.

"The officer told me to wait; he needed to talk to me. I had it in mind to just come clean with Mr. Hardman, though I hadn't actually done anything I could be charged with. I had to wait several hours while they booked Jed an' took him before the judge. That's why I'm late."

"I'm glad you're home. I . . . was worried."

"I knew you would be. I've given you reason to worry lately, Ellie, and I'm sorry. But I'll try not to give you any reason from now on."

Ellie felt warm tears of relief slide down her nose. "Wayne has done a lot for us, Jimmy. We've all got a lot to thank him for—before he leaves."

"If he ever wakes up." Jimmy ran his hand through his wind-vexed hair. "Is he any better?"

"Mazie came over today, and her baby pulled at his arm and tried to talk to him. He made an effort to open his eyes. He's going to be better; I feel it here." Ellie laid her hand on her bosom.

"Mr. Hardman asked if I would go over and tell the Greaveses that Jed is in jail. Would you mind so much doing it for me? I feel . . . uncomfortable around Jed's stepmother."

"I wouldn't mind at all."

Jimmy started into the house. "Oh, Ellie, I'm about to forget something, the reason Mr. Hardman detained me." He fished in his pocket. "Here. He said to give this to you with his apologies."

He dropped the brooch into Ellie's hand.

CHAPTER TWENTY-EIGHT
The Third Event

Three noteworthy things happened the next day.

Ellie, plagued with an unnamed restlessness, aroused before dawn. She went to Wayne's room, but he had not moved.

Framed in the doorway, she stood statue still, watching God create His morning, nudging the sun up and starting it across the blue sea of sky. A wind from the east began tearing the few gauzy clouds apart and scattering them. The birth of a new day always left her in a reverent mood.

At ten o'clock, a special delivery letter came for Ellie. When she saw that it was from Emil Samuelson, she dismissed the delivery boy with a thanks that barely masked her annoyance. Why should Emil Samuelson be writing to her? This was school's last week, and she had not gone back for private tutoring. Since Wayne's injury, she had been too busy to study. Mr. Samuelson was likely unhappy with her absenteeism. In his afflicted conception of life, nothing short of death itself should keep one from life's highest realm: book learning.

She tore open the envelope and saw that it was a lengthy letter. The small, stingy letters knotted and looped across the pages with maddening boldness.

"Dear Miss Webster," it began. "I had contemplated your presence for tutoring so that I might have a personal conference with you about the delicate matter herein stated.

"I find it regretfully necessary to withdraw my offer to support you financially in a marriage of convenience. Were the contract behind us, I would, of course, be bound to my legal obligations. But as nothing had been solidified, I find a nullification of my intentions justifiable.

"If I may exposulate: I have been presented with a cause even more compelling than your own. A friend of mine (of long standing), the former Wancille Aiken, is quite in need of personal protection. She is in a state of distress lest the man from whom she is estranged, a bigoted and selfish tyrant, return at an unsuspected moment and initiate bodily harm. She has interceded with me to provide for her the refuge she so sorely needs. This, my dear Miss Webster, would seem to take precedence over your own predicament, since you are in no immediate physical jeopardy.

"I hope that you will not be anguished, and I am happy to inform you that I have made other arrangements for your well-being. Wancille, her mother, and I have implemented an alternate plan for you that should sufficiently sustain you. I am confident that you will find it suitable. Wancille spoke to her employer about the possibility of transferring her job at the soda fountain to you. The wage is adequate for a singular individual such as yourself since you would have only your own needs to negotiate. The establishment will be pleased to give you a preemptive interview. Wancille's room just above the pharmacy will be available for your lodging, as well. I am delighted to be able to work out these details in your behalf."

Ellie's fingers tightened around the page, crumpling it. If this thoughtless, self-centered excuse for a man thought she would work in such a place—a place where shameless flirting met no deterrent—then he was gravely mistaken! She did not begrudge Wancille the man or his money. In some distorted way, they matched. But she did not need him to dictate her future. She tore the letter to shreds and dropped the pieces among the ashes in the stove.

She had promised Jimmy that she would get word to Mr. Greaves and Mazie about Jed, so she went to discharge that unpleasant duty, her mind still chafed by the gall of Emil Samuelson. Behind Mr. Samuelson's change of plans, she knew, was Beatrice. That's why Beatrice had hurried into town.

Mazie, not anticipating company, was still in her gown. The stench of the house reached out the door and assaulted Ellie's nostrils. But Mazie showed no embarrassment at the condition in which Ellie found her home.

"Lawsy, it's good to see you, Ellie," she babbled. "Please do come in. *Nobody* ever comes to see me. I get so lonesome and homesick I could just *die*."

A colony of sugar ants played follow-the-leader to a dropped half-eaten biscuit on the unswept floor. The worn linoleum gave no evidence it had ever been wet-mopped. Dirty clothes lay in rumpled heaps anywhere and everywhere. Moldy food disgraced the cabinet. There was no place to sit without sitting on rubbish.

Ellie's stomach gave a crazy lurch. She had never seen such disgraceful neglect. "Don't you ever clean your house, Mrs. Greaves?" she asked. To keep silent surely would be wrong.

"What's th' use? Greaves and Jeddy would just muss it again." She shrugged. "They don't care if I clean it or no. All they care is if they have another drink of their brew. An' why should I care if they don't?"

"But the baby could contact germs and get sick."

She sneered. "Babies *thrive* on germs. The sick 'uns are th' ones that are mollycoddled."

Ellie's repugnance fostered an idea. "Some day when I have more time, I'll come over and help you clean if you'd like."

"Would you *really?*"

"Why, yes. The lady who used to live here kept a spotless house. This is a *beautiful* little cottage. Do you sew? We could make some pretty curtains and a tablecloth to match."

"Naw, I never learned to stitch. Nobody never taught me. I warn't never *nuthin'*, Ellie. But you could mayhap teach me, couldn't you?" There was a wistfulness in her simple face. "I catch on pretty quick. Lawsy, that would be such fun—" She stopped and looked somber. "But I'm not sure I'll be here much longer. I'm beginnin' to just *hate* this place. And I think I'm beginnin' to hate Greaves, too. I'm thinkin' on leavin' him. Have you ever been around a drinkin' man?"

"No."

"Greaves hit me last night. An' it hurt. You can't cross a drinkin' man. They're mean as scratch an' have

The Third Event • 211

terrible temper fits. I been wantin' to go back to my mama. If I had just listened to her an' not married Greaves in th' first place. . . . He's *ages* too old for me. Lawsy, I'm young enough to be his *daughter.* . . ."

"But it wouldn't be right to leave your husband, Mrs. Greaves. You made a vow, and marriage is forever."

"But I didn't agree to live with a drinkin' man, Ellie. And I didn't agree to take on Jeddy, neither. He's right near as old as I am," she lowered her voice to a stage whisper, "and he's trying to *flirt* with me behind Greaves's back. I'd like to shuck both of 'um!"

"I came with bad news, Mrs. Greaves."

"Bad news? Did your hired hand die?"

"No, he's still alive. But I came to tell you that Jed is in jail. Mr. Hardman, the constable, sent word by Jimmy. He asked that we get word to you and your husband."

"In jail? Lawsy, Ellie! That's not bad news. That's *good* news! I don't know of a place on earth I'd rather him be. But what did he get hisself put in jail for?"

"You and Mr. Greaves should contact the officer and find out exactly what the charges are against him. I don't know the extent of it."

The glad light faded from her face. "It won't do no good for me to get my hopes all built up, Ellie. Jeddy an' his father are just like that." She held up two fingers side by side. "I *know* what Greaves will do. He'll take all th' money he has saved up to pay th' taxes on this place, and he'll bail Jeddy out of jail with that money. An' they'll go get theirselves drunk to celebrate. Then we'll have Jeddy back and no property to call our own."

"Surely he wouldn't do that."

"Oh, he sure would. Do you know, Ellie, that *anyone* could come along an' pay up those back taxes an' take over our place here, an' we'd have to move?"

"I'm afraid I know almost nothing about land laws, Mrs. Greaves."

"Then again," the light flashed back into her eyes, "I guess I'd be right glad if Greaves *did* lose this here place. We'd *have* to go back to Mama if that happened!"

And Mr. Samuelson will buy it for Wancille so she can be near her mother. Sickening thoughts, sights, and smells all merged.

Ellie wanted to flee the room, get to fresh air. "I need to get back," she said, holding back a wave of retching.

"You look poorly. Do you feel okay?"

"I'll be all right . . . when I get home."

"Wait! I found somethin' when I moved the bed in Jeddy's room to look for . . . for some money he'd lost. I remembered you saying that your boyfriend lived here, and I think he may have made what I found just for you." She hurried from the room in her normal shuffle and returned with a small heart, carved from wood and polished to a glossy finish. On it Daniel had carved his initials and hers.

Ellie gave a glad cry. "Oh, isn't it . . . beautiful! A little wooden heart!"

"You're so lucky, Ellie. If anybody in th' world ever loved me enough to make me somethin' like that, I'd go to my grave huggin' it. I'd never marry nobody else, neither!" With a hungering look, Mazie followed Ellie into the yard. "But I forgot to ask: is your hired hand gettin' better?"

"I'm . . . afraid not. But I'm praying, and . . . he will be."

"Well, here!" On an impulse, Mazie reached down to the big rosebush beside the front doorstep and picked the topmost rose from the shrub. Its petals, gilded about the edges, might have been painted by a famed artist. "Take this, and put it in your hired man's room for good luck."

Ellie took it and fled. Jimmy came out to meet her as she neared the house, "I think Wayne's worse, Ellie. He's really been thrashin' around. I'm afraid he may have taken a high fever. And, remember, th' doctor said fever wasn't a good sign."

Ellie rushed into Wayne's room, cringing when she saw the fever-spawned flush of his face. He opened his glazed eyes, and his unfocused stare searched the room. What was he looking for?

"Don't tell . . ." he mumbled in his delirium. Ellie moved closer to hear what he was trying to say. "Please, don't tell . . ." He repeated the fragmented request, his burning lips thick with unnatural sleep. Then he faded away again.

What is he trying to hide?

CHAPTER TWENTY-NINE

Laying down the Law

Beatrice was only gone two full days. She hired a phaeton to bring her back to the farm. Ellie wondered that she was home so soon and that her headache had miraculously disappeared.

"You're home." Mr. Webster's comment carried an unreadable quality. He kept reading the periodical he held in his hands.

"Yes! We've so much to do and so many changes to make!"

He said nothing.

"And in such a *short* time."

"Ummmmm."

"You heard me, didn't you?" Her words jabbed through the farm journal. "We've got a lot to do and a lot of changes to make in a *hurry*."

Mr. Webster lowered the publication slowly. "And just what changes are you talking about, Beatrice?"

"Oh, wait until you hear the good news, Ronald. It is just *too* wonderful! My daughter, Wancille, is to be wed.

She is engaged to the wealthy Emil Samuelson. Eleanor's rejection of his kind offer for marriage left him quite heartbroken. Wancille would have never been guilty of doing such a thing! And furthermore, my generous Wancille said that she would take Eleanor's place at the altar to save Emil the humiliation of cancelling all his plans. It was so *noble* of her, of course. Emil was so *humiliated* by Eleanor's rebuttal that he wanted a quiet little out-of-the-way ceremony, hidden from society's view. But I would hear none of his arguments. Nor would Wancille. *She* wasn't ashamed of Emil, she said, even if Eleanor was, and she wanted the world to know what a prize she was getting for a husband this time. We've asked the newspaper to publish it. We are planning a big celebration. . . ."

"We won't have a party here."

"Oh, I wouldn't think of having Wancille's reception *here,* Ronald. Not in this rustic place! What would my city friends think? We'll have it at the clubhouse in town, of course. That's where all society goes. I'll have to have a new ball gown."

"I've cancelled your charge privileges at Miss Judy's dress shop."

"Ronald, you *didn't!* I just must have a new outfit for my own daughter's wedding. As mother of the bride, it's unthinkable that I—"

"Wear the same one you wore to her first vows."

"Ronald! It wouldn't be proper. All my friends would think me cheap. Please don't insult me. Why, it's . . . it's not even the right color! But never mind the friction with Miss Judy. She's hard to get along with and is forever dunning her customers. She doesn't deserve my patron-

age. I found a *gorgeous* dress in the mail-order book while I was gone. Wancille likes it. I'll send off for it right away so that I'll have it in plenty of time for the festivities."

"Your mail-order credit is no longer good, either, Beatrice. Not under my name, anyhow."

"You can't do this to me!" Beatrice became angry.

Wayne groaned, and Ellie put a fresh, cold cloth on his fevered head.

"Don't tell me, Ronald, that the farmhand is still alive! Shakespeare said, 'There is a time to be born and a time to die.' This man is certainly taking his good time about dying, don't you think? How much longer must I put up with such annoying noises? And at a time when I'm supposed to be joyful, no less."

"You don't have to put up with anything, Beatrice. You are welcome to go back to your daughter and drink from your cup of joy to the full."

"Oh, but I can't go back to Wancille! We had words, and she sent me ho—"

"She sent you home, did she? I may just decide to send you right back to her."

Ellie was sitting where she could see Beatrice's painted face. A real fear crossed it. "I . . . can't go back, Ronald. She won't—" Beatrice stopped, diverting the stream of conversation, a ploy to humor Mr. Webster out of his sternness. "I do have some heartening news, though, Ronald! Since Eleanor won't be marrying dear Emil, we have decided on a very *wonderful* plan for her."

"What is your plan, and who is 'we'?" Mr. Webster's expression did not relax.

"Mr. Samuelson, Wancille, and myself. Wancille has

talked to her employer, and he wants to meet with Eleanor immediately. He says it is quite possible that Eleanor may have Wancille's good paying job *and* her living quarters in town. Eleanor is so handy in the kitchen. I *know* she can squeeze lemons! She's not bad looking, either. Now isn't that fortunate?"

"My daughter work as a soda jerk?" Mr. Webster's voice spun to a high pitch, razor sharp.

"Why, Ronald, why not?"

"*My* daughter will never work in a place like that!"

"How foolish! You do have such old-fashioned ideas! No wonder Eleanor is like she is. You have shielded her, denied her the pleasures of self-expression. You are absolutely *archaic,* Ronald. How shall she ever make her wage? Remember, I told you that no house is big enough for two women. Eleanor is working against the harmony of our household, and when I mentioned to her that one of us must go—"

"*You* told *Ellie* she must move out?"

"Not quite in those crude terms, of course, Ronald. She just—just *offered* to find another place to live so that we might realize greater peace here. As long as she is here, your devotion will be divided between the two of us. And . . . your sons *sabotage* my cooking. I have to throw out half the meal each evening, but they eat every scrap of food Eleanor cooks. It isn't fair to me."

Ellie had never seen her father's temper so explosive. He threw the magazine to the floor with a crash. "As Ellie's father, I shall provide for her until she marries!"

"But some girls never marry!"

He didn't even seem to hear her. "If it's between you and Ellie, then *you* will go!" he thundered. "And Ellie will *stay*. Who does ninety percent of the work around the place? Ellie! Who offers prayers every night for our souls? Ellie! Who nurses us when we're ill?" He jerked his thumb toward the sick room where Ellie hovered over the unconscious man. "Ellie, that's who! No man in his right mind would tell her to leave!"

"Why, Ronald, I've never seen you so . . . overwrought. You are in danger of having heart failure if you don't calm yourself."

"You haven't seen the half of what you shall," he said, leaning forward in his chair and pointing a threatening finger toward her face. "If you stay on here, there will be 'so many' changes to make. And in 'such a short time.' " There was something akin to mockery in his voice.

"What do you mean?"

"I mean you will clean up your babyish act. You will conduct yourself as an adult and accept responsibility."

"Where's my medicine? I feel a sick headache coming on right now, Ronald."

"Then take your medicine and *go!*"

"Where shall I go?" She began to weep.

"I have a 'wonderful plan' for you. Take Wancille's job as a soda jerk and live in her quarters in town," he spat. "That's what you suggested for my daughter."

"But, Ronald, I couldn't do that! Me, *work?* I've . . . never worked. Oh, please, don't put me out!" Her voice broke, and her body sagged like a sack emptied of its contents. "You don't want me. Wancille doesn't want me. Emil said I couldn't live with them. Nobody wants me. Oh, what shall I do?" Real tears rained down her face, smearing her makeup.

Her plaintive cry touched Mr. Webster. "You'll do as I say, then."

"Yes. Yes."

"You'll never have another headache."

"I promise. I'll never have another headache. It's—it's leaving right now. Yes, it's gone." She smiled to prove it. "Even without my medicine! Why, it's amazing. I—I doubt if it ever returns."

"And you'll never again complain about Wayne or the care my family and I are giving him. We all love Wayne however you feel about him. He's a prince of a man. If I decide to keep him on here forever, you are not to raise an objection."

"Keep as many dying people here as you wish, Ronald. I'll never say a word against Wayne again—sick, dead, or alive."

"You will stop spending money that we don't have."

"I'll stop. I'll wear the same old dress I wore to Wancille's first wedding. I can dye it and put a new collar on it, and nobody will recognize it at all. It will look absolutely elegant! Better than the one at Miss Judy's or the one in the mail-order book. I don't know why I didn't think of that at the start."

"And I'm bone tired of hearing you give credit to Shakespeare for what the Good Book says. Don't mention Shakespeare again. You'd do well to study the Bible, where your sayings are rooted."

"Of course, Ronald. If you wish—I didn't know—you see, I thought—"

"And we'll say grace at every meal."

"Of course!"

"And one more thing."

"Yes?"

"You are never to let me hear you belittle or ridicule

my daughter in any way. Ellie is a beautiful Christian, and she has been taught to respect her elders. She will not stand up for her rights against you, but she has a father that will. And you are to call her Ellie and not Eleanor. Her mother named her Ellie, and you will respect her mother's choice of a name for her."

"Why, surely, Ronald. You have my word that Eleanor will never be Eleanor again. She'll always be my little Ellie!"

"If you break the rules, you'll move in with Mr. and Mrs. Samuelson, *whether they want you or not!*"

When Ellie went to bed that night, she heard Willy and Walter whispering. "Did you hear what Paw told Beatrice, Walter? He told her if our way of life was rubbin' her fur th' wrong way, she'd best turn her cat around!"

CHAPTER THIRTY

Fevered Confession

The rose, plucked from Daniel's special bush, cheered Wayne's room. Ellie pledged that she would keep it alive as long as possible. She added a bit of sugar to its water. She hoped that Wayne would rally in time to enjoy its unique beauty.

For hours she had sat beside the man on the bed, bathing his face to bring down the raging fever, refusing her body the rest it craved. She studied his battered face. With the scars, his age was hard to determine. But his hair, a lovely chestnut color, and his voice revealed that he was still young. Probably somewhere in his late twenties. The distorted features had probably once been well situated. Some woman had been proud to call him her own. He was honest—and brave. What cruelty had life served this rootless man?

She knelt to pray as she had done every day since the accident. The doctor said the healing was up to a higher power now, the Great Physician. He had done all he could do. He held little hope for a complete recovery, but he encouraged the Websters to keep hoping and praying. "Sometimes they wake up all at once," he said. "And sometimes they die quietly in their sleep. We know so little about head injuries. I trust we'll see the day when we have great hospitals and can learn more about treating cases like this."

As Ellie talked with God, Wayne's eyes fluttered open, and a light of faint recognition crossed his vision.

"You . . . won't tell her?"

Of whom was he speaking? It was evident that there was a woman on the pages of his history. Suspecting it before, Ellie was now convinced. What secret did this mute man hold that he did not want told?

"Who?" she asked, trying to coax more conversation, more comprehension from him. If she could just bring his mind from the murky waters of unconsciousness! "What is it that you don't want her to know, Wayne?" Her voice, low and sweet, held womanly warmth. She must care for this helpless man as the one who loved him so dearly would have done, as she would have wanted someone to care for her own Daniel.

"Don't tell Ellie that . . . that . . ."

"That *what*, Wayne?" she pressed eagerly, laying her small hand on his arm.

What he was trying to say, she decided, concerned the icehouse accident. But if apologies were in order, she should be making them, not Wayne! She had been the one to bolt the door and trap him in the chilling atmosphere. However, knowing Wayne the little that she did, he would not want her to feel responsible for his injury, would not want her to carry the weight of guilt or remorse on her conscience. He was that kind of man. He would rather take the blame on himself, chalking it up to his own carelessness, than have her feel bad. He would say that he should have let someone know that he was in the icehouse.

Ellie tiptoed out of the room to find Travis. "Wayne is trying to say something," she told her brother.

"Really, Ellie? That's a good sign, isn't it?"

"I think so."

"You can't understand him?"

"He said, very plainly, 'Don't tell Ellie.' What do you think he means by that?"

Travis frowned. 'Now, that's strange. In all the time he has been here, I've never heard him call you Ellie. He always said 'Miss Webster.' I thought at one time that he had a case of the sweets on you. But when you never gave him any encouragement, . . ."

"I think, Travis, that he has a sweetheart or a wife, maybe even a child, in his past. And that . . . something happened to them. Did he ever mention them to you?"

"No, but I think you're right. He acted to me like a man with a heart not quite healed."

"Did he ever tell you how he got those scars?"

"No, Ellie, he never discussed them. He wouldn't have accepted my praise medals for bravery anyhow. Wayne is a very humble person. One of the most humble I've ever seen."

"Back during the snowstorm he mentioned to me something about losing the one he loved. I can't remember just now what he said. I think the scars have something to do with that tragedy."

"That's likely. It's funny about those scars. They bother him in some ways, and in other ways they don't bother him at all."

"You're not making sense."

"What I mean is, they don't bother him for himself. However he got them, he'd do it all over again without batting an eye. He just doesn't want other people to suffer at the sight of him. I never notice them myself. But I guess some do."

"I wish we knew a little more about him . . . about his background . . . about his family. . . ."

"I don't see that it would make a whit of difference. He's a part of God's family, and that's what counts."

"You're right, Travis. I just thought if I knew . . . her name . . . I could soothe him, answer his questions."

When Ellie returned to Wayne's bedside, he struggled to form more words. "Is she . . . here?" he asked.

She would have to tell him that the woman he called for was not in the room. His wife would not be coming to his side. It would not be easy. Her heart reached out to him, touched him, ached for him. If only she might find a way to comfort him, to ease his pain!

"She isn't here, Wayne." She said it with a quiet tenderness. "Your wife isn't here. I'm sorry."

"Then don't tell her . . . that . . ."

Ellie stroked his arm, tried to still his thrashing head. "We won't tell her, Wayne. Not if you don't want her to know. Rest now."

He struggled to finish his sentence. "Don't tell Ellie . . . that I'm *Daniel*.."

"But you are not Daniel," Ellie whispered. "Daniel is dead."

"Daniel didn't die," he groaned, throwing his head from side to side. "But don't let her know. I'm Daniel Wayne Brock. I . . . got my face messed up . . . under the hooves of the horses." He covered his face with his hand. "Mother, . . . I'm sorry I couldn't save you . . . . I'd never expect my little Ellie to . . . to love me . . . like this." His hand traced along the jagged scars and tried to cover the one bad eye. "I—I only wish I could have died in your place, Mother. But tell her . . . tell my Ellie . . . I won't ever cut down . . . *our tree.*"

CHAPTER THIRTY-ONE

Keeping a Promise

"Oh, Daniel, darling, I'm sorry!" Ellie was on her knees beside the bed, cradling his head in her arms. "I should have known by your voice, your kindnesses. But it's been so long. . . . I had almost forgotten. . . . Please get well, and I'll love you always!"

Unaware that he had revealed his identity, Daniel slept again with a peaceful smile. The fever died out that day, and he crept slowly back to the land of consciousness, urged on by Ellie's prayers that willed him to restored health. Her own Daniel was back, and she felt her heart would burst for joy!

She guarded her revelation, studying his twisted features for many hours. Yes, this was her Daniel. She could see it now. It was like the houndstooth check that played tricks on one's eyes; first it looked black on white, and then it looked white on black, but the material did not change, only the way the viewer saw it. How could she, blindfolded by her own grief, have failed to recognize her own Daniel?

Her heart brimmed with her secret, yet if a single person in the world knew, he or she might try to steal him away again. Not until Daniel got well would they reveal his identity. And they would be together when they made the revelation. Nothing must separate them now.

Every scar was a thing of beauty to her. He had risked his life to save his family, and these were his trophies. Had a woman ever been prouder of a man? She would spend the rest of her life admiring these marks of honor.

When Wayne woke to full cognizance, he followed her everywhere she went with his good eye. She hummed about, wreathed in a halo of happiness. Her dream lived again, and that was all that mattered!

"You are working too hard...for me, Miss Webster," he protested. "I'm not...worth it."

The time was right. No one was in the room to disturb the moment of disclosure. She laid her slim hand on his brawny arm and felt it quiver at her feminine touch. *"Daniel Brock,* you are worth all the world to me. I still love you, and I always will! I'll never let you go away without me again!"

He reached for her hand, his own trembling. "My little Ellie. My precious little sweetheart, do you mean it? But how did you know? Who told you? I didn't mean for you to ever...find out."

"Your heart spoke out loud while your mind was unconscious."

"Did it? Well, what an incorrigible heart! I was afraid something like this might happen. Do you really love me like this?"

"Oh, I do, Daniel!"

"But look at me...my face. I..."

Ellie put a finger softly over his lips. "Shhh. Don't ever say it, Daniel. Those are scars of bravery, and . . . I'll always think they are beautiful. I'm proud of every one of them! Oh, Daniel! If you had just told me when you first came, . . ."

"I almost broke down during the snowstorm while I was sleeping in the attic. I could hardly bear your sweet nearness. In fact, I started you a note, writing with my left hand so you wouldn't recognize my penmanship. But I—I couldn't finish it."

"Why, Daniel?"

"I—saw my reflection in the dormer window, and it reminded me that you—deserved—a better looking face—your children deserved a better father with two good eyes. Something better than this." He put his hand over the chewed-up ear.

"Daniel! The reflection you saw was an outside view of yourself. It's the inside that counts! And that part of you hasn't changed at all. You're just as honest and noble, you're just as precious to me, as you were six years ago." She laid her cheek against the handsome scars and then raised her head and looked directly into his good eye. "What woman or child could ask for anything better than love?"

He gave her his best lopsided smile. "I've lived six years to hear those words.

"It won't be any problem to get my land back for . . . us, Ellie. I've kept up the taxes all these years. All my family was—murdered—and I'm the only Brock left to claim it. I was glad to see that the rosebush is still there." He gestured toward the wilting rose in the bud vase. "My 'Ellie bush.' And I planted us a big garden and cut us enough firewood for a couple of years. You went to town with me the other day when I talked to the land man. He said that I could have the Greaveses off the land within a week. I'm the legal owner."

"Oh, I'll—I'll be so glad when they are gone. Mrs. Greaves isn't caring for your—for our little house."

"I noticed."

"It makes me heartsick to see it dirty." She shook her head as if to erase the thought of the cottage's filthy condition. "And Mr. Greaves drinks."

"The Greaveses haven't been good for—any of us. The day you fainted at the well, I almost lost my—victory— over that Jed."

"How did it happen that you were at the well that day?"

"I've never been far from you, Ellie."

"The day I went to care for the baby, you knew I was there?"

Daniel chuckled. "I followed you there—and back. I knew there would be trouble."

"And you," Ellie laughed and cried intermittently, "you took the heart off the wall."

"I couldn't stand his initials linked with yours. You were too . . . pure."

"Thank you, Daniel. I couldn't bear it, either."

"The devil planned a heyday with you in the house alone." He winked the good eye. "I like to interfere with the devil's plans. I had to fight off the . . . enemy . . . several times. The night Julius tried to snow you—"

"You knew about that?"

"I was just outside the window. I've known Julius for years. I knew he was married. If he had tried anything,

I'd have come right through that window! And Mr. Samuelson . . . you weren't still planning to marry that—that mealy-mouthed character, were you?"

"Mr. Samuelson spared me the decision. He decided to marry Beatrice's daughter."

"The one who works at the drugstore?"

"Yes. Wancille."

"I don't know which of the two deserves my pity—or prayers—the most."

"The day the baby was sick you almost gave yourself away in the barn, didn't you?"

"I came frightfully close!"

"When you said, 'Open your mouth for Da-', I thought you had started to say 'Daddy.' I hadn't any idea 'Daniel' almost slipped out. I supposed that you had lost a wife and a baby through some misfortune. I stitched up a whole story from that half yard of fabric!"

"You did, didn't you!"

"Did you see the rose I left in the barn?"

"Yes. I knew it was from my 'Ellie bush.' I shed so many tears that I—I couldn't come in for supper with my red and swollen eyes."

"A lot has happened in these last few days, Daniel. And it's all because of *Wayne*. Jimmy has done an about-face. He broke off with Jed. And just in the nick of time. Jed is in jail."

"Jed in jail? For what reason?"

"For theft. He's the one who put the whiskey under the seat in our buggy that Saturday."

"I—I was planning to get your mother's brooch back for you."

"Mr. Hardman sent it back. He caught Jed up to the

same mischief again. Jed saw our buggy in town and thought it was you—and me—and planted another bottle there to cause us trouble. Except this time he got caught."

"He's always been jealous of me, Ellie. He—sensed—that I loved you."

"I should have sensed it, too! It's permissible for love to be blind, but when it's *dense* . . . !"

"If you hadn't been so much in love with Daniel Brock, you might have caught on to Wayne's secret. But what else has happened?"

"Beatrice quit having headaches." Ellie giggled.

"Now that's truly a miracle. But tell me, do we have to endure her cooking until . . . until I get well enough to marry you? If so, I'll stay with the broth, please."

"We don't have to endure anything we don't want to. Paw is making the rules now. Beatrice is like a lamb."

"How did that happen?"

"He told her to shape up or ship out. Wancille won't take her. Her son won't have her. Mr. Samuelson doesn't want her. If she doesn't march to Paw's drum, she doesn't march at all. The boys are loving it!"

"If she can come under subjection to your father, Ellie, she might learn to come under subjection to God. And in that case, there's hope for her salvation."

"I hadn't thought of it just that way, but I saw her reading the Bible last night."

"Travis and I prayed a lot of prayers for her. And remember, my love, God hasn't lost the pattern to *any* of our lives."

Ellie's eyes glistened with happy tears. "He hasn't, has He?"

"And about the letter you found in the house: I had

no idea it never reached you. My kid brother, Aaron, was supposed to have posted it. I thought it had been mailed. Why, you must have thought I had deserted you!"

"I didn't know what to think. I was . . . confused."

"My poor darling! My reason for returning here and hiring out to your family was to claim you for my own. But when I got here and saw how lovely you had become, I couldn't . . ."

"Where were you going when Paw laid you off?"

"Not far. Unless you had decided to marry . . . someone else."

"And you would have let me go the rest of my life not knowing who you were?"

"I was praying about it, Ellie. This—this was His way of working it all out. I am grateful to whoever locked me up in the icehouse."

"I'm afraid I did it."

"Thank you. And I'm . . . sorry about the tree."

"Were you really going to chop down . . . *our* tree, Daniel?"

"No. I heard you coming down the path and raised the axe on purpose—to see if you still . . . cared." He stroked her cloud of golden hair.

Ellie gave a musical laugh, the first in six years. It rang like a clear-toned bell. "And you found out how much I care, didn't you, my darling?"

He pulled her close. "Remember the day I carved that heart on the tree? I said that next to God, I loved you best and that someday I would marry you and we would be together forever?"

"I could never forget."

"I plan to keep that promise."

She laid her head against his chest, thrilling to each heartbeat. Now she had more than a wooden heart.